"Nine short st̲_____ress
such topic_____d
first love _____er
dialogue cl_____er
novels, suc_____
Desperate [_____cholastic
paperback]. —Horn Book

"The short story — ironic, at times satiric and
poignant — is too little used in young people's
books. Mrs. Conford succeeds with stories
grounded in human sensitivities and brightened by her sure knowledge of what makes
people laugh." — The New York Times

"Beginning frenetically and continuing at a
nearly hysterical pitch, these nine stories
deal with the anguish of being a teenager...."
— School Library Journal

"This collection of nine short stories is fun to
read as romance and humor abound in typical
Conford fashion. The heroines are normal
teenagers who have problems...yet manage
to solve these problems without compromis-
ing their self-identity. Fast-paced, easy reading, this collection will appeal to Conford's
fans and win her new readers. Recommended
for all collections. — Voice of Youth Advocates

**Other Scholastic paperbacks
you will enjoy:**

Anna to the Infinite Power
by Mildred Ames

Dear Lovey Hart, I Am Desperate
by Ellen Conford

Jock and Jill
by Robert Lipsyte

Run, Run, as Fast as You Can
by Mary Pope Osborne

Sarah Bishop
by Scott O'Dell

Seven Days to a Brand-New Me
by Ellen Conford

A Smart Kid like You
by Stella Pevsner

*We Interrupt This Semester for
an Important Bulletin*
by Ellen Conford

If This Is Love, I'll Take Spaghetti

Ellen Conford

SCHOLASTIC INC.

New York Toronto London Auckland Sydney Tokyo

ISBN 0-590-32338-5

12 11 10 9 8 7 6 5 4 3 2 1   8   4 5 6 7 8 9/8

Printed in the U.S.A.   01

For
Pat Scales

Friend of readers
Friend of writers
Friend of mine

Contents

If This Is Love, I'll Take Spaghetti

If This Is Love, I'll Take Spaghetti

*P*izza," I moaned. "French .... fries. Chocolate graham crackers. Big Macs. Thick shakes. Eclairs. Spaghetti and meatballs."

"Carrot sticks," said Judy. "Celery. Green pepper strips. An eight-ounce cup of bouillon."

"You don't offer a drowning man a glass of water!" I cried. "I can't stand it anymore. I've got paper cuts all over my fingers from opening those bouillon packets. If I eat one more carrot stick I'm going to turn yellow. That can happen, you know. Too much Vitamin A makes you turn yellow. *Listen to me.* I've got to have something that doesn't crunch when I eat it or I'm going to die."

"Bouillon doesn't crunch," Judy pointed out. "And you're not going to die. You've got to stop thinking about food all the time. You've got to put food in its proper place. It's just not that important."

"When you've got enough, it's not important. When you're starving—"

"You're not starving. You're on a perfectly

adequate diet of twelve hundred calories a day, and no one starves on that."

"I do!"

It was true. I'd only been on the diet three days, but I was ready to throw in the sponge. (Sponge cake. Devil's food cake. *Pizza*.) The doctor had given me that "perfectly adequate diet" and told me I could expect to lose two pounds a week. Since I had to lose twenty pounds, that meant ten weeks of carrot sticks, bouillon, and broiled chicken.

"I'll never make it."

"Of course you'll make it," Judy said. "I have faith in you."

"I don't know why. I never made it any of the other times."

This wasn't the first diet I'd been on. I'd been overweight ever since sixth grade, and every attempt at losing my excess poundage had been a dismal failure.

I'd tried the grapefruit diet, the kelp diet, the Miracle Alfalfa diet, the Beverly Hills Diet, the Scarsdale diet, the Oshkosh diet—if it was written up in a magazine, or had "miracle" in its name, I'd tried it.

Nothing worked. By the second day I'd get discouraged. By the third day I'd be depressed. By the fourth day, visions of Mallomars danced in my head.

So I always ended up saying, "What's the use? I'll never lose all that weight." Looking at myself in the mirror and knowing I'd never look the way I wanted to depressed me so much that the only way I could cheer myself up was to eat an entire box of chocolate chip cookies.

After which I got depressed all over again because I hated myself for eating an entire box of chocolate chip cookies. And what was the point of going back on my diet when I'd already ruined it by eating all those cookies?

"This is different," Judy said. "Everybody knows crash diets don't work. Those others were all faddy things. This is the first time you've tried a normal, sensible diet. I mean, look at all the things you're allowed to eat."

"Are you kidding?"

The doctor had given me this mimeographed list with two columns of food on it. The first column was headed "Foods to Avoid." The second column was "Permissible Foods." The first column had about a hundred things in it, ninety-eight of which I love. The second column had about fifteen things in it, and every one of them was either bland or *blecchh*.

"Somehow I can't work up a whole lot of enthusiasm because I'm allowed to eat all the kale I want."

"Why don't you stop thinking about the food you're not allowed to eat and start thinking about something really important?"

"Like what, for instance?"

"Like Jeff Nugent, for instance."

"How come," I asked, "when you say that all I can think of is Fig Nugents?"

"Cut that out! Look, you're the one who's madly in love with Jeff Nugent. You're the one who—"

"I never said I was madly in love with Jeff Nugent! I said I found him mildly attractive."

"You said—and I quote—'He makes my toes curl.' You said, 'If only I could lose twenty pounds—' "

"You know what, Judy? At this very moment, if you said I could have my choice between Jeff Nugent and a bowl of spaghetti and meatballs, I'd take the spaghetti. It isn't worth it. Not for Jeff Nugent, not for *any* boy."

"What about for yourself?" Judy asked quietly. "Are *you* worth it?"

I hesitated. "I never thought about it that way before."

"Well, think about it. You don't have to lose

weight for me to like you. You don't have to lose weight for your parents to love you. And for all I know, you wouldn't have to lose weight for Jeff Nugent to be interested in you. The question is, how do *you* feel about you?"

I didn't answer. The truth was too depressing.

....

No thin person can ever understand the torture of loving to eat and hating to be fat at the same time. All the circles in my math book reminded me of pizzas. How could I concentrate on my homework when all I wanted to do was draw anchovies and mushrooms on it? Triangles looked like ice cream cones. And it certainly didn't help that half the problems involved *pi*, which equals 3.1419. I kept thinking, "Blueberry *pi* r squared . . . *pi* r squared à la mode."

By dinnertime I thought I was going nuts. (I wasn't allowed to eat them, either.) I went to the kitchen to set the table and looked at the picture of Cheryl Tiegs I had taped to the refrigerator. (The idea was, every time I was tempted to open the refrigerator, I would see thin, gorgeous Cheryl, and that would motivate me to look like her, which I could only do by *not* opening the refrigerator.)

My little brother, Barry, had erased her eyes

and drawn little red dots in her eyeballs and fangs
sticking out from her mouth.

She still looked better than I did.

We sat down to dinner.

"My, my, doesn't everything look delicious,"
my father said encouragingly.

"I know what that green guck is and you
can't make me eat it," Barry threatened.

"Oh, goody, kale again." I was too weak from
hunger to make myself sound as sarcastic as I felt.

"Just because *she's* on a diet," Barry said,
"why do *I* have to eat this crummy stuff?"

"It's not crummy stuff," my mother said.
"It's healthful, nourishing food. We're all eating
more sensibly thanks to Jamie's diet."

"I'm not," said Barry, pushing his plate
away, "because I'm not eating."

My father pushed the plate back. "If you
don't want to eat the kale, don't eat the kale. But
there's nothing wrong with the chicken or the
baked potato or the salad."

Barry held his nose. "I can't eat anything
with this green gunk all over my plate."

My father jumped up and got a clean plate.
"Here," he snapped. He put the chicken and the
potato on the clean plate, and took away the one
with the kale on it. "Now keep your mouth shut
and eat."

"How can I eat with my mouth shut?" Barry asked.

"Barry," my mother warned.

Another pleasant family dinner. "I'm sorry to cause all this trouble," I said softly. "It doesn't seem right for everyone to suffer just because I—"

"First of all, nobody's suffering," my mother said.

"I am," Barry whispered.

"Second of all, you're not causing any trouble. And third of all, even if you were, it's worth it."

Was it?

I looked down at my plate. Even though I was weak from hunger, the sight of a naked baked potato with no butter melting into it, no sour cream oozing over its little bumps and dripping into its little crevices, did nothing to perk me up.

The broiled chicken breast looked nice, but it was so *dry.*

The only thing that was moist or otherwise juicy was the kale.

We won't discuss the kale.

I looked over at my mother's plate. She had butter on her potato. My father had butter *and* sour cream. Barry was mashing his up with butter and a little milk from his glass.

I took a mouthful of dry potato. I washed it down with a sip of 99% fat-free milk.

Is it worth it? I wondered. Judy's question echoed in my mind. Am *I* worth it?

I still didn't have an answer. And what happened the next day didn't make the question any easier.

••••••••••••••••••••••••

I was in the supermarket, picking up a few things for my mother. I personally thought that sending a dieter to the supermarket constituted cruelty to fat people, but my mother had to work late and I didn't want to give her a hard time.

I was reaching for a container of fat-free milk when a voice behind me hissed, "Not that one. Take one of these."

I turned around, and there was Jeff Nugent, in a white apron, standing over a plastic crate of milk cartons. He thrust a container at me.

"Jeff! What a—uh—surprise."

Which was putting it mildly. I didn't know whether to be thrilled that I'd run into Jeff like this, or embarrassed because he saw I was buying fat-free milk. I certainly would rather have run into him in the cat food aisle, but we don't have a cat.

I wanted to say, "Oh, this fat-free milk isn't for me, it's for my mother," but that would have been a little obvious. As it was, I couldn't think of a thing to say. Not with him standing so close to me so unexpectedly. My stomach did something funny—and it had nothing to do with hunger.

"See, this is the fresh stuff," Jeff said confidentially. "That stuff on the shelf is going to be outdated in about five minutes."

"Well . . . thanks." I took the container of milk from him. The tips of our finger touched. The carton slipped out of my hand and fell into the shopping cart. There was a sharp *crack* and several softer crunches as it hit the carton of eggs on the bottom.

"Uh-oh," said Jeff. "I think I broke your eggs."

"No, no, it's my fault."

He reached into my cart and took out the egg carton. Little drips were beginning to seep out the sides. "Shh," he said. He took the eggs down the aisle, picked up another carton, and stuck the broken ones way in the back of the display.

"Well, thanks again," I said as he put the eggs in my cart. There was nothing else I had to get, but I didn't want to leave. I smiled because I couldn't think of anything to say, and he smiled back, sort of shyly. I think my toes may have curled.

"I—um—didn't know you worked here. I mean, I'm here all the time and I never saw you before." I was babbling, I knew it. Why did I have to say that about being in the supermarket all the time? I could almost hear him thinking, Well, no wonder you're so fat.

"I just started last month," he said. "And I only work from four to nine on school days, so I guess our paths just never crossed before."

How romantic that sounded! Our paths never crossed before . . .

"Did you do the reading for English yet?" he asked. "I didn't even get a chance to look at the assignment, but it sounded like a lot of pages."

"Well, it's just poems, so it's not that much."

Jeff made a face. "Ugh. Ten pages of poems. I hate poetry. I can never understand it."

"It's not so bad. There are pictures on a lot of the pages, so there's not that much to read. But it must be hard, being here till nine and then having to start on homework."

"Yeah, kind of. Especially homework I don't understand." He looked at me sort of shyly. "You're really good in English, aren't you?"

My heart began to thump, and I got this funny tingly sensation on the back of my neck. Was Jeff hinting around, working up to asking me for help in English? Or was he just making conversation? If he was just making conversation, *why?* Why was he standing here talking to me when he should have been unloading milk crates or stacking cottage cheese or raising yogurt prices?

I gripped the handle of my shopping cart hard, hoping that would keep me from showing all I was feeling.

"If you want . . . I mean, I'd be happy to— I mean, if you're having trouble . . ." I just stood there and stammered. And tried to uncurl my toes.

"Would you?" His face lit up. His adorable, sweet, shy face. I was suddenly light-headed, and I knew this wasn't from lack of food either.

"Sure." My voice sounded squeaky. "You could come over after work if you want."

"It wouldn't be too late?" He looked so pleased, so eager, so hopeful. Could he be *that* excited about getting help with the assignment? Or was that look on his face because *I* was going to give him the help?

But how could that be? How could Jeff Nugent, the cute, want to snuggle up to Jamie Wade, the plump, and discuss Robert Browning (the poet)?

Maybe, I thought wildly, my diet has worked already. Maybe I'm not fat anymore.

". . . yeah, nine-fifteen's okay. See you then."

Dazed, I checked out my stuff, practically sprinted home, and ran upstairs to weigh myself.

I'd lost one pound.

Could one pound have made that much of a difference?

. . . .

"It's crazy," I told Judy on the phone. "He *does* like me. I mean, he's been here four times and we only spend about fifteen minutes on the homework. The rest of the time we just talk. I mean, I really think he likes me."

"I think he does, too," said Judy. "It sure sounds like it. So what's so crazy about that?"

"He wasn't supposed to like me until I lost twenty pounds. What does he see in me?"

"What do you mean, what does he see in you? You're nice, you're fun, you have a good personality—and twenty pounds overweight is not exactly like being an elephant, you know. Don't look a gift horse in the mouth."

"I wish you'd stop talking about meat," I sighed.

"Still hungry?"

"I'm *always* hungry. You know, it's a myth that being in love takes away your appetite."

"Yeah?" Judy laughed. "Remember when you said if you had a choice between Jeff and a bowl of spaghetti, you'd take the spaghetti? Would you still take the spaghetti? . . . Jamie? Jamie? Didn't you hear what I said?"

"I'm thinking, I'm *thinking*."

....

I didn't have to make a choice.

The next week Jeff suggested we go to the movies. And after the movie we stopped at McDonald's. I hesitated only a second before deciding that a Big Mac and a thick shake were just what I needed.

I took one bite of the Big Mac and one sip of the shake and fell off my diet with a crash. I'll make up for it tomorrow, I told myself. I won't eat a thing tomorrow. Or Monday either. I know there are five million calories in a Big Mac and ten million in a thick shake. So I won't eat Tuesday.

But at that moment, with that first ambrosial taste of gloppy sauce and pickle and lettuce, with that first nectar sip of a thick shake . . . it was heaven. Of course, food always tastes better when you eat it with someone you love.

Especially if you've been starving for ten days.

On Sunday, Jeff asked if I wanted to go to the nature preserve at the state park. How romantic, I thought, walking through a deserted forest of bare trees in November, just the two of us . . .

It was wonderful. Jeff casually took my hand in his, and, when the wind picked up he sort of held me against him so I wouldn't be blown away. I was hardly thin enough yet to be blown away—especially after last night's binge—but maybe Jeff saw me that way. Maybe I didn't look as heavy to him as I did to myself.

You know, you can work up a whale of an appetite walking for miles through a deserted forest in November. The way I figured it, I must have walked off at least a million of the calories I'd taken in last night, so when Jeff wanted to stop to get something to eat, I agreed enthusiastically.

After all that good exercise, I hardly felt guilty about wolfing down my fish and chips. (Fried. Both on the "Forbidden" list.)

· ·

I spent the rest of the day alternating between moods. After Jeff dropped me off at home, I mooned around my room for about half an hour, replaying the soft kiss he'd given me at the preserve, just before we went for fish and chips.

Then, for the next hour, I hated myself for eating the fish and chips. I felt guilty, stupid, weak.

Which made me hungry.

I went downstairs to the kitchen and yanked

the refrigerator door open. I looked inside, then slammed it shut. I glared at the picture of Cheryl Tiegs. I imagined I saw reproach in her eyes. (Which was silly, because all she had in her eyes were those little red pinpoints that Barry had drawn.)

"Jamie," I could hear her saying, "how could you? Don't you want to look like me?"

I ripped the picture off the refrigerator door.

"Why should I want to look like you? Jeff likes me just the way I am. He doesn't care if I lose twenty pounds or not. And the only reason I started this stupid diet in the first place was because I thought he'd notice me and like me if I was thin. Well, I'm not thin and he likes me, anyway. So I don't have to lose weight for Jeff."

And then, eerily, I sort of imagined Cheryl's voice and Judy's voice blending together, and this combined voice said, "What about for you, Jamie? What about for yourself?"

. . . .

"You know," I told Judy on the phone, "it's very hard to diet and to be in love at the same time."

"You mean, you still can't decide whether to dream about Jeff or spaghetti?"

"Well, sort of. But what it really is . . .

every time I think about Jeff I can't help thinking about all that food I eat when I go out with him. So I start to feel guilty and then I start hating myself and then I can't think about Jeff anymore."

"Sounds to me like what you really mean is it's hard to be in love and *not* diet. If you stuck to your diet, you wouldn't feel guilty and hate yourself, and you could dream about Jeff all you wanted."

"If I stuck to my diet I'd probably be too hungry to dream about Jeff. I'd be dreaming about hot fudge sundaes. And besides, I don't want him to know I'm on a diet."

"The way you're eating now, he'll never know, that's for sure."

"Thanks a lot," I said sourly.

"But why would he have to know?"

"What am I going to say if he asks if I want a Big Mac?"

"How about 'no thanks.' Or is that too simple?"

"But what if he asks how come? I mean, all of a sudden I don't like Big Macs?"

"Tell him you're not hungry."

"Listen, Judy," I said bitterly, "a good relationship is not built on lies."

••••••••••••••••••••••••••

I struggled through the rest of the week battling hunger pangs. I was back on my diet again, but it didn't seem to be any easier. I tried substituting thoughts of Jeff kissing me for thoughts of spaghetti, french fries, and devil's food cake, but it didn't work too well. As I saw it, the problem was that I knew I could have my devil's food cake and Jeff, too.

But for some reason, I felt this determination to stick to my "Permitted Foods" list. Maybe it was like punishing myself for the binge I'd had over the weekend, but whatever the reason, by the time Jeff and I went out again the next Saturday, I'd lost three pounds. (I was sure it would have been four if I hadn't slipped off the wagon.)

We went to a party at one of Jeff's friend's houses, and along with the usual potato chips and stuff there was this huge, five-foot-long hero sandwich. You just cut off a piece for yourself whenever you get hungry.

I looked at it longingly. There were all kinds of good things in there. Cold cuts, cheese, olives, peppers, onions . . .

After we'd danced a couple of times, Jeff said, "Let's have some of that sandwich. I'm really starving."

I looked at the hero and I looked up at Jeff.

Even slow dancing works up an appetite—well, let's face it, *anything* works up my appetite—and that huge hero was about the most tempting thing I'd faced in two weeks. (Except, of course, for Jeff.)

"Isn't that a great idea?" he said. "A five-foot hero sandwich? Only, it's not five feet anymore. I think there's only about two feet left. Come on, Jamie, I'll cut us off a couple of pieces."

Oh, why not? I asked myself. It's a party. It's special. Just this once. I'll make up for it tomorrow. I won't eat a thing tomorrow. How often do I get a chance to help demolish a five-foot hero sandwich?

"No," I said, before I even realized I was going to say it. "No thanks, Jeff. You go ahead and get a piece for yourself."

"You sure?" he asked doubtfully.

I'm sure that I made those same excuses for gorging last week. I'm sure that I'll hate myself if I eat so much as a mouthful of that sandwich, just as I hated myself all week for the Big Mac and the fish and chips. I don't want to hate myself anymore.

"Yeah, I'm sure."

Jeff came back with a big chunk of the sandwich. "It's fantastic," he said. "Here, try a bite."

I turned my head away quickly, before I could get a good whiff of the strong cheese, the pungent peppers, the fragrant oil . . .

"I can't, Jeff," I said bluntly. "I'm on a diet."

"On a diet? What for?"

"To lose weight. I have seventeen pounds to go."

"I mean, why do you have to lose weight?"

"Oh, come on, Jeff," I said impatiently. "I'm twenty pounds overweight. At least, I was. Don't pretend you didn't notice."

"I'm not pretending *anything*. I like you just the way you are."

"Oh, Jeff . . . that's such a nice thing to say." I felt my heart melting and hoped it didn't mean my determination was melting, too.

"I'm not just saying it. It's the truth. To me you look . . ." He hesitated a moment, then said shyly, ". . . really good." He took a big bite of his hero and chewed hard.

"But to me I don't."

That was it, I realized. That was it in a nutshell. Jeff may like me just the way I am, but I don't. And I didn't want to hate myself anymore. Not for the way I ate, not for the way I looked.

I wasn't losing twenty pounds for Jeff, or for

the doctor, or for my mother or for anyone except myself. I knew the answer to Judy's question now. I'd probably really known it all the time.

"You're the one that counts," Jeff said. "If it's important to you, that's what matters. I think it's great you have that much will power."

"Oh, Jeff, I don't!" I wailed. "It's so hard. I mean, right this minute I want to rip that sandwich out of your hands and wolf the whole thing down before you can grab it back."

Jeff grinned. "You just try it, Jamie. Just try it."

"You wouldn't let me?"

"Not if you don't want me to. You helped me with poetry, didn't you?"

"You mean, you'll help me with my diet?"

"If it's what you want," he said, "I'll help you any way I can."

"Oh, Jeff." I looked into his eyes. He was gazing down at me so gravely, so intently, I forgot all about hero sandwiches and potato chips and stupid, unimportant things.

I sighed.

"Oh, my," I murmured. "I think you're helping me already."

I'll Never Stop Loving You, Tommy Toledo

I've always considered myself a very level-headed sort of person. While my friends struggle through adolescence alternating between moods of rapture and despair, I sail along on a fairly even keel, never—or almost never—going overboard about anything.

If my hair doesn't look exactly right after I blow it, I don't feel tempted to walk around with a paper bag over my head, like my friend Sheila does. I just stick a flower or an enameled comb in it and go about my business. If I don't have a date for New Year's Eve, I don't contemplate becoming a nun. If I fail a math test, I don't assume it will mean that I'll never get into the college of my choice and will end up selling potato peelers at Woolworth's.

And while many of my friends flit from crush to crush, falling madly in love with a different rock star or actor every week, I've always preferred to concentrate on *real* people, instead of fantasizing about media creations I'll never meet.

"Isn't he gorgeous?" Sheila will say, clutching a magazine cover with a picture of her latest idol to her heart. "Doesn't he give you goose pimples?"

"He's attractive enough," I usually reply, shrugging.

"*Attractive?* Is that all you can say?"

"That's all he *is*. He just doesn't do anything for me."

"Nobody does anything for you!"

Which was true.

Until Tommy Toledo came along.

Tommy Toledo leaped into the public eye—and my heart—when his first single, "You Make Me Crazy," from his album, *New Kid on the Block*, broke all records and became the number-one song in the country three weeks after it was released.

When I first heard the song, it didn't make much of an impression on me. The lyrics, as far as I could understand, were something like:

You make me crazy, ooh, ooh, ooh, both day and night,
I once was lazy, now I'm uptight,
I feel neurotic, uhh, uhh, uhh, and out of touch,
It's hypnotic, the way you make me love you so much.

The beat was pretty good, and though his backup group—bass, drums, piccolo, and barrel organ—was a little bizarre, the arrangement was certainly interesting.

But nothing to get excited about.

Until I saw Tommy Toledo's picture on the cover of *Persons* magazine.

I was in the supermarket buying milk, bread, and Hot Dog Helper for dinner (it was my night to cook), when I saw it in a magazine rack.

I stopped dead at the end of the express line. A woman behind me hit me in the back with her cart (which had twenty items in it, easily), but I hardly felt it.

TOMMY TOLEDO—HIS RECORD BREAKS RECORDS!

And his face, gazing out at me from the cover. Black hair, parted in the middle, curving soft waves over his forehead; deep, soulful brown eyes, searching, searching . . . for mine?

Almost in a trance, I reached for the magazine and put it down on the counter next to the Hot Dog Helper.

. . . .

"Katie, I just don't know what you see in him."

We were at Sheila's house, studying for a biology test. We were supposed to be quizzing each other. What we were doing was looking at the pictures of Tommy Toledo; Sheila for the first time, me for the forty-seventh.

"He used to be a pinball addict," I said dreamily. "Can you imagine? He once played eighty games of pinball in a row."

"I don't see why that impresses you so much. You don't even play pinball. Katie, what's gotten into you?"

"That's how he met his band. They were all perfect strangers who happened to come together in one of those inexplicable, mystic moments of karmic conjunction."

Sheila peered over my shoulder. "You're reading that right out of the magazine," she said. "No wonder he's got such a weird group. I mean, piccolo and *barrel organ?*"

"And he doesn't need stage gimmicks, like blowing up his amplifiers or biting the heads off live chickens or chewing beer bottles."

"I'm relieved to hear it," Sheila said. "Listen, have you memorized that whole article? I hope you know your biology that well."

"Just good, solid sound, with lyrics that make a statement, that speak to the hearts and minds of today's youth culture."

"He doesn't speak to me," Sheila said. "Katie, I've never seen you like this. And over *Tommy Toledo?*"

I closed the magazine. "Listen," I said passionately, "did I ever make fun of any of the crazy people you had crushes on? Did I laugh at you when you fell madly in love with Walter Cronkite?"

"I didn't fall madly in love with him!" Sheila said indignantly. "I said I admired him as a father figure."

"Same thing. Just disguised a little."

"It certainly is not! I—"

"And when you were ready to hitch to Nashville to try to meet Wailing Wally Pflugg, did I make fun of you? Even though he looked like a cross between a mass murderer and a goat?"

"He did not look like a goat!" Sheila cried. "And yes, as a matter of fact, you did make fun of me."

"And Faron Monday, with all his hair shaved off except for one inch down the middle of his head? Not to mention Burt Reynolds, Robert Redford—"

"Well, what's wrong with them?" Sheila asked. "Plenty of people think they're handsome."

"But you come up with a new one every week," I said. "You're fickle. You always think you're in love, but they're just crushes, like all the kids have. Now this—"

"This isn't a crush?" Sheila asked sarcastically.

"No. This is the Real Thing. I'll never stop loving Tommy Toledo."

"Oh, sure."

"Let me ask you a question. Have I ever said that before about anyone?"

"No," she admitted.

"There you are. That's the difference between you and me. *You* have childish crushes. *I* am finally tasting the bittersweet fruits of true love."

"You," said Sheila, "have finally gone off your gourd."

••••••••••••••••••••••••

I bought every magazine and newspaper I could find with features on Tommy Toledo. There began to be quite a few of them as the weeks went by. Every time I was in the supermarket, there would be an issue of the *Midnight Inquirer* or the *National Star Reporter* with a front page headline about Tommy Toledo.

TOMMY TOLEDO'S SECRET ANGUISH!

TOMMY TOLEDO—"WHAT I WANT IN A WOMAN!"

THE UNTOLD STORY OF TOMMY TOLEDO'S TERRIFYING BRUSH WITH DEATH!

And the magazines: *Pop World, Rock Reporter, Star Track*. All of them had big stories—with lots of pictures—about Tommy Toledo, just as "You Make Me Crazy" was making music history.

" 'A sensationally successful media blitz'," read Sheila, " 'is turning a mediocre singer with a ragtag assortment of instrumentalists into a show-biz phenom. Tommy Toledo (who comes from New Jersey) started a whirlwind promotional tour this week with a sold-out concert in—of all places—Toledo.' Mediocre singer," Sheila said. " 'Ragtag assortment of instrumentalists.' Media blitz."

"Isn't that an adorable picture of him?" I sighed, and began ripping the page out of the magazine.

•••••••••••••••••••••••

I got a bulletin board and some push pins, but I soon ran out of space on it for all the pictures of Tommy Toledo I'd collected. I began sticking them up all over my room with Scotch tape.

Of course, I bought the album, just as soon as the record store got it in. There was a picture of Tommy on the cover, walking down a city street at night, and spray-painted on a brick wall was the title: NEW KID ON THE BLOCK.

He was all dressed in white satin, with his guitar slung over his shoulder.

He was beautiful.

His songs were interesting, too. The more I listened to "You Make Me Crazy," the more I realized how truly meaningful the lyrics were. And most of the other cuts were just as good: "I'm No Gorilla, I'm a Man"; "Don't Grow Up To Be a Banker Like Your Daddy"; "Doin' Eighty on a Street Marked Thirty-five"; and "Ooh, What You Make Me Feel Like."

I called my parents into my room to listen to "Doin' Eighty." The words to that one were particularly good, I thought. Very symbolic and meaningful, all about Life, not just driving.

When it was over, my father, who *claims* to be a music lover, said slowly, "You know, I have a feeling if I could understand the lyrics I'd really hate them."

My mother said, "Did I hear a *piccolo* in there?"

"He's very innovative," I said. I could tell they didn't really appreciate him.

There are some things you just can't share with your parents.

And then one day I read a little item, practically buried in the newspaper gossip column. "Tommy Toledo, top teen tunester, will be taking a bite out of the Apple next week. He'll do one concert at the Regent but will spend most of his

time on the talk show circuit plugging his best-
selling debut album."

"He's coming here," I breathed. I closed my
eyes and held the newspaper to my heart. "*Here.*
My prayers have been answered."

Then I ran to the phone to call Sheila.

"He's coming to New York!"

"I guess I don't have to ask who," Sheila said.
"When? Is he giving a concert?"

"Next week, and yes, at the Regent. Oh,
Sheila, I'm going to get to meet him at last!"

"What do you mean? There'll be hundreds of
kids at that concert. Don't ask me why—there's
no accounting for taste. How are *you* going to get
to meet him?"

"I'm not sure yet, but I will. I *have* to. This
is fate, karma, destiny. All these weeks I've been
dreaming of a chance like this, and here it is! It
was meant to be, there's no other explanation."

"There are nine million people in the New
York metropolitan area, and he's coming here to
meet *you?* It might not be to get news coverage, to
push his album, to make money on a concert?"

"Well, naturally, that's what he thinks he's
coming here for."

"My, my, isn't he in for a surprise. And how
are you going to work this miracle?"

"I told you, I don't know yet. Of course, it won't be at the concert."

"Of course not."

"Oh, Sheila, we'd better find out where to get tickets! Before they're all sold out."

"What do you mean, *we?*"

"You're coming with me, aren't you? I mean, you're my best friend. Don't you want to share this . . . this spiritual experience with me?"

I thought I heard Sheila snort. Then there was a pause and she said, "Listen, Katie, when I wanted to hitch to Nashville, did you offer to go with me?"

"Hitching to Nashville is not exactly the same as going into the city on the train for one night," I pointed out. "And besides, you didn't ask me to."

"Well, after you said that was the stupidest thing you ever heard in your life and you wouldn't be caught dead within a hundred miles of that creepy-looking Willie Pflugg, I didn't think there was much point in asking you."

"Sheila, I need you. My happiness is at stake. My parents will never let me go to that concert alone."

"All right, all right. But I thought you said you weren't going to try to meet him at the concert?"

"I'm not. But I have to *be* there, don't I?"

"I guess so. Boy, Katie, you're acting so weird. I'll be relieved when you're over all this and back to your normal self."

"I'll never be over it," I vowed. "I'll never stop loving Tommy Toledo."

I dragged Sheila to Ticketron the next afternoon on the off chance that they would be selling tickets to the Tommy Toledo concert. The woman said they had just gone on sale yesterday and were going like hotcakes. She expected to be sold out by the end of the day.

"Oh, Sheila, aren't we lucky? Just think, if we'd waited one more day we would have lost out."

"Funny, that's exactly what I was thinking," Sheila said wistfully. "Katie, do you realize this ticket is costing me three weeks' allowance? Not to mention the train fare . . ."

"I know. I wish I could treat you, but—"

"Never mind, never mind. You'd do the same for me, I suppose. Unless it meant going to Nashville."

•••••••••••••••••••••••••

I began to buy every newspaper on the stands, scouring them for information on Tommy Toledo's New York tour. I needed to know what shows he'd be appearing on, on what days, and, most importantly, where he was staying.

Day after day I came home with an armload of newspapers, spread them out on the living room floor, and tore through them, page by page, looking for any mention of Tommy Toledo.

"Why this sudden interest in current events?" my father asked.

"I like to keep up."

He watched me for a moment, running my finger down the page, flipping to the next page, running my finger down that one, and so on.

"Nobody can read that fast," my father said.

"Actually I'm just skimming."

"Nobody can *skim* that fast."

I even bought the *Wall Street Journal,* just to cover all bases, and the Spanish language newspapers, figuring that I'd certainly recognize the words "Tommy Toledo" if they had a story about him, and if they mentioned his hotel or the talk shows he'd be doing, they'd obviously be the same as they would in English.

"That's in Spanish," my mother said, looking over my shoulder.

"Reading a newspaper is a very good way to practice a foreign language."

"But you take French," my mother said.

"They didn't have any French newspapers."

Finally, two days before the concert, I found it. Again, buried in the gossip column. "Tommy Toledo and his entourage have booked the entire tenth floor of the posh Champlain Hotel for their three-day stint in Gotham. A far cry from the pinball days, eh, Tommy?"

"Eureka!" I shouted, leaping up from the floor.

My mother eyed me curiously.

"Uh—sorghum prices have leveled off," I stammered.

"*There's* good news," she said.

I ran upstairs to call Sheila.

"The Champlain Hotel," I said. "Do you have a Manhattan directory?"

"And hello to you, too," she said. "Yes, why?"

"Look up the address, will you?"

"Okay, but why?"

"It's part of my plan."

"What plan?"

"The one I'm still working on. Sheila, do you realize I'm everything he wants in a woman?"

"How do you know that?"

"From the article I read about 'What I Want in a Woman, by Tommy Toledo.' I'm sympathetic, understanding, have a good sense of humor, am vitally concerned with world peace and the plight of the poor and downtrodden——"

"Oh, come now!"

"Sheila. Just look up the address."

· ·

By the night of the concert I had the whole plan worked out. As I explained to Sheila on the train into the city, it was really incredibly simple.

"As soon as the concert's over, what does everybody do?"

"Go home?" asked Sheila.

"No. They rush around to the stage door and wait for Tommy Toledo to come out, hoping they'll get his autograph. And what do we do?"

"I give up."

"We zip over to the posh Champlain hotel, stroll casually into the lobby, and take the elevator to the third floor."

"The *third* floor?"

"Right. This is a really clever plan. We get out at the third floor and no one suspects we really want to go to the tenth floor. Then we find the service stairs and walk up."

"*Seven flights?*"

"Right. It would be a lot easier if we had a blueprint of the Champlain, but we'll manage."

"Seven flights?"

"Right. Then when we get to the tenth floor, we wait on the landing. We don't go into the hall yet, just in case they've got security people there. Now, I figure after the concert they'll go some place to eat and sort of unwind, you know, and they ought to be back at the hotel in a couple of hours. So when we hear the elevator stopping—"

"A couple of hours?"

"Yeah. Well, two, two and a half at most. But it probably won't even be that long, because he's got all those tapings tomorrow—"

"Katie, my folks'll kill me if I get home later than one."

"Didn't I tell you to say you'd be late?"

"One *is* late! You don't know what I had to go through to get them to agree to *that.*"

"All right, all right, we'll call them from the city and tell them we're going to be unavoidably detained, so they shouldn't worry."

"*I'm* going to to be unavoidably detained," Sheila said miserably. "In my room. For the next month."

"Sheila," I said, grabbing her hand, "you know how important this is to me. This could change my *whole life.*"

"Mine, too," she said. "Like, into death."

• •

I was so excited by the time the concert started, I was ready to die. It wasn't only that I was finally going to see Tommy Toledo in person, which would be thrilling enough in itself, but knowing that in just a few short hours I'd be talking to him, meeting him face to face. I got chills just thinking about it.

We had to sit through an extremely boring set by some unknown group called Dr. Denton and his Original Electric Nectarine Band. The Regent was packed. Every seat was taken, and even though they were obviously there to hear Tommy, the audience was very polite to Dr. Denton. They even applauded after each number. Some idiot actually yelled, "More!"

"Is he crazy? They've been on an hour already!"

"They're very good," Sheila said, clapping loudly.

"Stop clapping!" I cried. "They'll never get off!"

But they finally did.

And the audience started clapping and stomping and chanting, *"We want Tommy! We want Tommy!"*

The house lights went completely dark for a moment, and then, suddenly, there was a flash of blue-white light, and there he was, in the middle of the stage, all dressed in black with TOMMY spelled out in rhinestones on his shirt.

"Ohhh!" I moaned. I slithered down in my seat. "I'm going to faint."

"Put your head between your legs," Sheila advised.

"It's too much . . ."

"I think so, too. I think it's positively tacky."

Everyone was screaming and yelling when the band started the lead-in to "You Make Me Crazy," but they quieted down when Tommy started to sing.

I didn't scream. I just leaned my head back against the seat and took deep breaths while his beautiful, tender, soulful voice sang—it seemed—only to me. He was practically staring right at me.

"I'm going to die," I declared.

"I'm going to barf," Sheila said. She had to yell to be heard over the sound, so I may have misunderstood her.

He sang all the songs from *New Kid on the Block,* plus two new ones, and by the time the last encore was over I was limp as a noodle.

We were sort of carried along by the tide of people rushing to the exits; outside it seemed as if the whole surging mass was spilling around the corner to the side of the theater.

"See," I said weakly, "I told you. They're all going to the stage door to wait. Now we'll go up one block and catch a cab. My plan is working perfectly so far."

We didn't have any trouble getting a taxi, and as we settled back in the seat and I told the driver, "Champlain Hotel," I actually got goose pimples.

This was it! Phase One of Operation Toledo was successfully under way. In just a couple of hours—maybe even less—Tommy Toledo would gaze into my eyes, recognize that I was a kindred spirit, and not just another silly, infatuated teenager, and—

"No gimmicks," Sheila snorted. "Just good, solid sound—"

"What are you talking about?"

"That article in *Persons* magazine. What a laugh."

"Why? It *was* just good, solid music."

"Oh, yeah? What about the cherry bombs?"

"He was using them like exclamation points, you know, for emphasis. He was making a statement."

"He was making *noise*," Sheila said. "And what about when he tore his shirt off, threw it on the floor, and jumped up and down on it?"

"It gets hot under those lights," I said.

"Okay. All right. What about when the organist took off his shoes and played the organ with his feet. What do you call *that?*"

"Sheila, that's show biz!"

"I give up." She sat back in the seat and folded her arms.

"Here you are," the taxi driver said. He pulled up at the entrance to the hotel.

"That was fast," I said with a nervous little laugh.

"Terrific," muttered Sheila. "Do you realize it's already eleven forty-five?"

I paid the driver and a doorman opened the cab door for us and helped us out.

"Thank you," I said, trying to sound gracious, and trying to look like I was used to walking into posh hotels, particularly this one.

"I think you're supposed to tip him," Sheila said when the doorman made no move to open the lobby door for us.

"What for?" I pushed the door open boldly, and we walked into the Champlain Hotel.

Even though it was late, there were quite a few people in the lobby. Most of them were very dressed up. My heart began to pound so loudly I was sure someone would hear it.

"This isn't going to work," Sheila hissed. "Anyone can tell we don't—"

"Shut up and keep walking," I whispered. "They can't possibly keep track of all the people staying here. Everything's going fine. All we have to do is find the elevators." I sounded a lot more confident than I really was. Any minute now I expected a tap on the shoulder from the doorman or the desk clerk or a policeman—someone who'd demand to know what a couple of scruffy-looking teenagers were doing at this hour in the lobby of the posh Champlain Hotel.

"Going up! Going up!"

"There!" I said. "Come on. Don't run. Look nonchalant."

We walked, nonchalantly, to the elevator. I stepped in behind a woman in a white fur coat, who said, "Seven."

"Three, please," I said. It came out like a little squeak.

The elevator man glanced at us—just for an instant. I thought my knees would buckle under me. Then a few more people got in the elevator, and he didn't pay any attention to us. The door closed with a smooth swoosh, the elevator rose.

I barely had time to think, Phase Two, successful, when the elevator stopped and the man announced, "Three."

We were the only ones to get off, and even though I stumbled as we stepped out into the hall,

I think we looked pretty nonchalant. At least, the door closed right behind us, the elevator was gone, and no one seemed in the least suspicious.

Sheila leaned against the wall and closed her eyes. She looked sort of pale.

"Sheila, we made it! The hard part is over. All we have to do now is find the stairs."

She groaned. "And climb up seven floors."

"But we're out of danger! No one will catch us now. Who uses stairs in a fifteen-story hotel?"

She opened her eyes and glared at me. "Only idiots like us."

We wandered around the third floor, looking for a staircase, and finally found a door with a red EXIT sign over it.

"That must be it. Come on."

"We should have left a trail of breadcrumbs or something," Sheila said. "We'll never find our way back from here."

"Oh, don't worry," I said confidently. "We'll be able to come down all the way in the elevator. Once I've met him we won't have to sneak around anymore."

The first two flights weren't bad, but Sheila needed to rest after the third. I felt fine. I was so excited I must have had extra adrenaline or something. "We did it! I'm going to meet him at last!"

"Yippee," Sheila whimpered.

I could have bounced up the next four flights, but Sheila was so tired I climbed up very slowly so she wouldn't feel she was holding me back or anything. I was sure we had plenty of time before Tommy got there.

When we finally reached the tenth floor, Sheila sagged against the railing and sort of flopped down on the top step.

"Eureka!" I whispered loudly. "It went like clockwork! I told you! Oh, Sheila, this is destiny! This was meant to be! Our lives are inextricably wound together in one of those mystical karmic—"

"Katie?" Sheila panted.

"What?"

"*Shut up.*"

••••••••••••••••••••••••

Every ten minutes Sheila looked at her watch and said, "Do you realize what time it is now?"

"Ten minutes later than the last time you told me," I kept saying. "I'm sure he'll be here any minute now. Oh, I can't stand it!"

"Katie?"

"You're not going to tell me what time it is again, are you?"

"No. I was just wondering about something. Why was he standing on that box?"

"What box? He wasn't standing on a box, that was a platform. Lots of performers use them."

"Yeah, but the rest of the group was standing right on the stage. You know, lots of times they have platforms at different heights, or the lead singer is on stage level and the rest of the group is on platforms. Don't you think it's kind of unusual? And did you notice, he never once got down off the platform? I mean, not even to run offstage at the end of the show. He just stood there till the lights went down."

"So? What are you getting at?"

"Well, picture him in your mind."

I closed my eyes. "Mmmm," I said dreamily.

"Standing there, on that box—"

"Platform."

"Platform . . . with the rest of the group around the stage?"

"Yeah. So?"

"Are you visualizing it?"

"Yes," I said impatiently. "I'm visualizing it. What?"

"Where does his head come to?"

"*What?*"

"In relation to the other members of the group," Sheila said, "who are standing on the floor, remember. At what level is his head?"

"About the same as theirs. So?"

"Katie, how tall are you?"

"Five seven. Why? Oh, Sheila, honestly, you mean he's short? Is that what you're trying to say?"

"Katie, he's not just short—he's *short*. If the average height of the group is five nine, and that platform was—"

"Oh, Sheila, how can you be so shallow? What difference does height make? In that whole article about what he wants in a woman, he didn't once say she had to be short. There are far more important things in life than size, you know. Love is not measured with rulers."

"Very well put," Sheila said.

"Thank you. I thought so."

"I just didn't want you to be—uh—shocked or anything. You know, you've built this into such a big—"

"Sheila! *Shh!*"

I clutched at my heart and leaned my ear against the door. We hadn't even opened it to scout around, because we were afraid there might be a security guard posted on the floor, and if he saw us, it would be all over.

Through the door I could hear loud voices, laughter, somebody singing.

"You must be crazy, ooh, ooh, ooh, to buy this record, uhh, uhh, uhh . . ."

"It's *him!* Sheila, this is it! I can't stand it! I'm going to faint. I can't open the door. Sheila, open the door. No, don't, I can't go through with it, I think I'm having a heart attack. Sheila, *open the door before it's too late!*"

She opened the door and we lurched out into the corridor.

There he was, coming right toward us. Tommy Toledo, my true love, my eternal love, looking magnificent in a black cowboy hat and a down flak jacket. His band members were right behind him, along with two other guys I didn't recognize.

He stopped short. So did his entourage.

"How did *you* get up here?" he demanded.

Before he could say anything else, before I could chicken out, I grabbed Sheila's arm and ran toward him.

"Oh, Tommy," I said breathlessly, "I just had to meet you. We were at your concert, and even before that, I mean, I just had to tell you——"

I didn't realize I was looking down at him until he tilted his head back to look *up* at me. Then I saw he couldn't have been more than five feet two inches tall.

"Whoo, you're a big one, aren't you?" he said.

"Well, actually, I've got these really high

heels on, and—" I pointed to my shoes, but he'd turned toward Sheila, who is four inches shorter than me.

"Hey, baby, you're just about right." He leered at her. "Are you a fan of mine, too?"

My mouth dropped open. How could he do that? How could he turn his back on me, on fate, on destiny, on a true soulmate? How could he grin like *that* at Sheila, who couldn't stand the sight— or sound—of him? This isn't fair, I thought, this isn't what's supposed to happen. My plan was working so perfectly. How could it go wrong now?

"Tommy, please, listen, I'm the one who—" Was I crying? I don't remember. I might have been.

He took a step toward Sheila. "What's your name, honey?"

He was ignoring me completely.

Sheila began to get red in the face, and when she finally spoke, the words came out in jerky little gasps.

"You are a clod—and a creep—and have *very bad manners*. The only reason *I'm* here is because she . . . she . . . I never wanted to go to your concert. I never wanted to meet you. She's your biggest fan. Except for yourself. You—you can't measure love with a ruler. And you're the *worst singer I ever heard*."

"Hey, you little—"

They all started toward us, and Sheila grabbed my hand and ran, pulling me to the stairway door. She pushed it open, pushed me through it, and we raced down the ten flights of stairs, not stopping once till we reached the bottom.

....

Even though it was three A.M. when we got home, I couldn't go to bed until I had ripped every single picture of Tommy Toledo off my walls.

The next day, Sheila and I burned them, one by one, in her fireplace.

Tommy Toledo's newest record, "Never Stop Loving Me," was just released, and it's already in the Top Ten.

It's a stupid song.

I turn off the radio every time it comes on.

············

What
Do I Do
Now?

············

*D*ear Dr. Lamour,
•••••••••••••••••• I never thought I'd be writing to you about romantic problems. Since I've never had any romance to speak of, I never had any romantic problems to write to you about.

But here I am, writing to you because you've helped so many people and I really don't have anyone to turn to in my time of need. Which this is.

Actually, I don't have a romantic problem yet. The problem is that I don't have a *romance* yet. And I want one. A particular one, that is.

His name is Alvin. He sits next to me in geometry—my worst subject! He never says a word to me. Sometimes he nods when I sit down in the morning, but that's about it. The thing is, I think I'm madly in love with him and I don't know what to do about it.

I know it's probably hard to believe that I could be madly in love with someone named Alvin, but "What's in a name?" as Shakespeare said. (I think it was Shakespeare. It may have been Gertrude Stein.)

Anyway, I am an extremely shy person, and since he never speaks to me, I don't know how to get him interested, even if he *could* be interested in me, which he might be if I could only say something witty or clever, which he would have to answer or, at least, smile at.

So far all I've been able to do is say hi, and that hasn't exactly bowled him over, and why should it, because hi is not a very witty or clever remark. (That's when he just sort of nods.)

Anyway, I don't know what to do about this. If he didn't sit right next to me, I guess I would just worship him from afar, but he's not afar, he's right there, and who knows what might happen if I could just get him talking?

So my question really is, I guess, how do you get a boy who never talks to you to talk to you, when you haven't got anything to say to him except, "I'm madly in love with you," which, of course, I could never say. I mean, I'm *really* shy.

Hopefully yours,
Extremely Shy Person

Dear Extremely Shy Person,

I'll bet Alvin is every bit as shy as you are! I'll bet that's why he hasn't said anything to you. For all you know, he's as interested in you as you are in him! But you'll never know if neither of you ever tries! Since you're having trouble with geometry, why not work up your courage and ask him to help you with the homework? That gives you a good excuse to "break the ice" and talk to him. He might just be waiting for you to make the first move! And, as a bonus, you might even learn geometry!

Dr. Lamour

Dear Dr. Lamour,

You remember I wrote to you about Alvin, the boy who sits next to me in geometry? You told me to ask him to help me with my homework, since I am so bad at geometry.

Well, that may have sounded like an easy thing to do. I mean, it was a very ingenious and sensible suggestion, because if I asked him a direct question like that, I knew he'd have to answer. And if he just nodded, like he usually does, that would mean yes!

But, remember, I am very shy and not good at talking to people, and when you said I should "work up my courage," you said it exactly right. Because that's what I had to do.

Three days in a row I went into class, sat down next to Alvin, and tried to open my mouth to say, "Boy, I really need help in geometry. Could you help me?"

Finally, on the fourth day, I gave myself this really stern "pep talk" before geometry, and I went in and sat down next to Alvin, and was just about to "take the plunge" when Ms. Fromberg, our teacher, handed back Monday's test papers.

I got a 52 and thought, This is it, this is the perfect chance to ask Alvin for help. So I turned around to talk to him, and saw, just before he stuffed it into his notebook, *his* test paper, with a big 36 circled in red at the top.

What do I do now?

Hopelessly yours,
Extremely Shy Person

Dear ESP,

The situation isn't as hopeless as it seems! After all, since Alvin is doing as badly in geometry as you are, you have something in common! That's a "plus" in any relationship. And misery loves company, you know! Why not tell Alvin about the trouble you're having with this subject? Then he'll probably tell you about his problems with it, and before you know it, you've got the conversational ball rolling!

Dr. Lamour

Dear Dr. Lamour,

I don't know if you remember me, but I wrote you about this boy I'm madly in love with who's also failing geometry and you told me to talk to him about my trouble with geometry to start the "conversational ball rolling."

Well, the most awful thing happened!

When I came home from school the day I got the 52 on the last test, my parents got really upset, and when we figured out my average, we realized I would probably fail for the marking period, so my parents got me a tutor.

And the tutor is really good—better than my teacher, in fact—and she's been working with me for three weeks now and wouldn't you know it? All of a sudden, all those things I didn't understand, I started to understand. It was just like in the cartoons, when a light bulb goes on over a person's head.

So on the last two quizzes we had, I got a 9 and a 10. (Which is the same as 90 and 100 on a big test.) So now I can't talk to Alvin about how badly we're both doing in geometry because I'm doing great, and if misery loves company, I can't be company for him anymore.

I have the rottenest luck in the world!

Now Alvin looks at my test papers, and his

test papers, and just sighs and sticks his in his notebook. He probably hates me!

I don't know *what* to do now!

Despairingly yours,
Extremely Shy Person

Dear Extremely,

You could be of great help to Alvin in his time of need. Sometimes the best way to get over your own shyness is to help someone else who needs help.

Since Alvin has noticed how well you've been doing in geometry, why don't *you* offer to help *him?* He'll be doubly grateful: not only for the help you can give him but for showing that you're interested and you care.

Just work up your courage and try it! Good luck!

Dr. Lamour

Dear Dr. Lamour,

It's me again.

I'm sorry to keep bothering you like this, but really, everything seems to go wrong for me, and I just don't know who else to turn to.

I mean, it's not bad enough that I'm an extremely shy person, it's not bad enough that I'm now passing geometry, it's not bad enough that I fell madly in love with someone who will probably never be interested in me, but to top it all off, I read these letters you get from people who are so grateful for the help you've given them and tell you their whole lives have changed because of your advice, and I wonder, How come you give me such good advice and nothing ever works?

Remember how you told me to talk to Alvin about how well I was doing in geometry now because of the tutor? Well, like you said, I "worked up my courage." (That took two days. And on the third day, I had to give myself another pep talk.)

Anyway, the third day I was determined to talk to Alvin, especially since we got another quiz handed back, and I got a 10 and Alvin got a 3.

So before he could hide his paper away in his notebook, I took a deep breath and said, "You know, I was doing really rotten in geometry, too. And then my parents got me a tutor, and I've gotten 9's and 10's on all the quizzes ever since."

And Alvin finally said something to me.

You know what he said?

"Must be a very good tutor."

I was so excited that he was talking to me at last that I just blurted out, "Oh, she is, she's terrific. Much better than Ms. Fromberg."

And he said, "Could you give me her phone number?"

What could I do?

I gave him her phone number.

Why am I doing everything wrong? Why isn't this working out like you said? You give such good advice to everybody else, what's the *matter* with me?

And what in the world should I do *now?*

Desperately yours,
Extremely Shy Person

Dear Person,

There is nothing the matter with you that a little self-confidence wouldn't cure! You don't really need a "gimmick" to get a boy to pay attention to you. You just have to be brave enough to take the risk of showing that *you're* interested in *him.* Your mutual difficulties with geometry made a good starting point, but it's not the *only* starting point.

There's more than one way to "skin a cat." Or start a relationship. Why not give a party and invite Alvin? Why not ask his opinion on the upcoming elections? And there's still geometry. You might even suggest studying together, now that you're both working extra hard on it.

You give up too easily!

Dr. Lamour

Dear Dr. Lamour,

I know it's been a long time since I wrote to you, and I really meant to write sooner to thank you for all your help and advice about my problem, namely Alvin who sits next to me in geometry.

You were very patient about answering all my letters and giving me such good suggestions. I'm really grateful that you took all that time and trouble with my "small" problem, when there are so many people out there who write to you about divorces and alcoholism and compulsive gambling.

But I did want to let you know what happened, because I thought, Who knows? Maybe someone else with the same problem will see my letter if you print it, and realize what Dr. Lamour can do to help *them*.

Well, after my last letter to you I thought about the advice you gave me. As I am an extremely shy person, I was afraid that giving a party and asking Alvin to come when we'd hardly ever exchanged two words to each other might seem a little pushy, and besides, to tell you the truth, I didn't have the nerve.

I guess I was afraid if I did invite him, and he said no, I'd be so embarrassed and upset I wouldn't be able to concentrate in geometry for the whole rest of the year, what with him sitting right next to me and me knowing he didn't like me. And now that I'm running an 85 average in geometry, I'd really hate not to be able to concentrate in class!

Then I thought about your suggestion that we discuss the elections, and I realized that if I asked his opinion about the candidates, and he told me, I'd have nothing to say back, because I didn't know the first thing about the elections, except that everybody says that one of the candidates for state senate from our district is a crook, but that's only political mudslinging, I suppose. But the thing is, I really wasn't interested in the elections, which I suppose is very irresponsible and un-American, but I'm too young to vote anyway, so I just didn't get involved. How could I start a discussion on a topic I couldn't discuss?

That left studying geometry together.

Well, if I couldn't work up the courage to ask Alvin to a party where there'd be not just him but lots of other people, I certainly didn't have the nerve to ask him to come to my house and study geometry with me. Alone! I mean, I just *couldn't*.

But that gave me an idea.

My tutor, Mrs. Lee, was helping me prepare for the midterm exam, going over all the stuff that I'd been failing in the first few weeks of the semester, when I asked her if Alvin had ever called her.

She said yes he had, and she'd seen him three times already.

So I said, "He's sort of nice, don't you think?"

And she said yes, but kind of introverted. (So I guess you were right about him being as shy as I am!)

And I told her maybe she hadn't noticed, but I was really introverted, too.

So she said, "Yes, I noticed," and sort of smiled. She's really a very sweet person, along with being a terrific tutor.

And then this light bulb went on over my head again.

"You must be very busy this time of year," I said, "what with everybody cramming for midterms and all."

And she said she was, and it was hard to arrange her schedule to accommodate everyone.

"Well," I said, "you could double up. I mean, like, for instance, Alvin and I are in the same class, and we're studying for the same midterm, so you could tutor us both in the same hour and make the same amount of money in one hour instead of two."

And she sort of grinned again and tilted her

head and asked, "You think that would be fair? The point of a tutor is to provide one-to-one instruction."

And I said, "Yes, I know, but you've been such a good tutor, you can see I don't need that much help anymore. With *geometry,* anyway."

Her eyes kind of twinkled knowingly. And she thought about it for a little while, and then said, "Well, I guess it would be all right just *once.*"

"Just once is all I want," I said.

So she set up a session at her house, telling Alvin it was necessary this one day that she work with two students at the same time. He told her he didn't mind because he was doing so much better since she'd been tutoring him, and if the *other* student needed more help than he did, that would be okay.

It wasn't till he got to her house that he realized the other student was me!

Mrs. Lee sat us side by side at her dining room table and gave us some proofs to do, and told us if either of us got stuck we could ask the other for help, and to see if we could work out the problem together.

Neither of us got stuck on the first two proofs. By the third one, I was getting a little worried. Alvin still hadn't said anything to me except a kind of startled hi when he walked in the door and saw me. This whole hour could be wasted if something didn't happen soon.

I looked sideways at him. He was staring down at the third problem. Just staring. His pencil wasn't moving. I looked at the proof. And then I got this weird feeling that *he* was staring sideways at *me*.

"Boy," I said nervously, "this is a tough one."

Alvin cleared his throat and mumbled something.

"Maybe we ought to work together on this one?" I said it fast but in such a little, timid whisper I didn't think he heard me.

"Okay," he said. "It's really hard."

So we started working on it, and all of a sudden we found we were talking to each other, telling each other how to do the proof!

And we started laughing, and I finally gasped, "I really knew how to do that problem."

And Alvin was laughing so hard he nearly tilted his chair over backwards onto the floor, and he said, "So did I!"

Anyway, it's not exactly a "big romance" yet, since Alvin and I are both very shy people, as you know, but things look very promising. We're studying together almost every day (without Mrs.

Lee!) and I think Alvin really likes me, although of course he's too shy to come right out and say anything very romantic. But that's okay, because so am I!

I just wanted to tell you what a big help you've been and how I never could have done it without you! It's good to know I can turn to you whenever I have a problem and know that you'll help me out, no matter how many times I have to write to you and vice-versa.

Gratefully yours,
Extremely Shy (but happy!) Person

Dear Ex,

I'm always delighted to be of help. But do me a favor? Next time, try Mrs. Lee first.

Dr. Lamour

Take My Mom — Please!

I felt sorry for Tamara Cherp the first time I saw her. Even before I knew her name was Tamara Cherp I felt sorry for her. Oh, there's nothing wrong with "Tamara"—it's a sort of exotic-sounding, romantic name. But Tamara *Cherp?*

It was the first day of our first year in high school, so all us freshmen were kind of floundering around in a state of general confusion. The school seemed huge, and there were a lot of sadistic sophomores who seemed to enjoy misdirecting us when we asked how to get to our rooms.

I got to my last class of the day, which was Spanish, feeling generally frazzled and practically friendless. The high school takes kids from four different areas, and though I knew there were kids from my old school in there somewhere, I'd hadn't seen a friend all day.

A girl stood in front of the door to 412 looking up at the room number and down at her schedule card. She kept shaking her head.

She looked as confused as I'd felt most of the

day, but that wasn't why I felt sorry for her. It was the way she was dressed.

She wore a yellow T-shirt with a picture of Mozart on the front—I only knew it was a picture of Mozart because underneath the head it said MOZART—a shapeless black skirt that drooped halfway down her calves, and a black leotard. A red scarf wound around her forehead like an Indian headband. The ends hung down over one ear.

I couldn't imagine why she was dressed like that, unless she'd just arrived here from another planet. No one dresses like that in our school. She looked bizarre, and I was sure she'd had an even more miserable day than I did. I may have been a timid, floundering freshman, but at least I looked like all the other timid, floundering freshman. No one pointed or stared or snickered as I walked down the hall; I was sure they must have at this girl.

"It *says* 412," she said. I didn't know if she was talking to me, because she was still looking back and forth from her schedule card to the door.

"Then this must be the place," I said. "Spanish One?"

"Yes, but this boy told me I had to go downstairs, past the main office, through the gym—"

"One of their little jokes," I said wearily. "It's happened to me twice today. I think this'll be

the only class I'm not late to. And that's only because I had English in 410 last period."

"Oh."

We went into the classroom and sat down at
adjoining desks. The room was only about one-
third full. I knew that people would be straggling
in for a good ten minutes after the bell rang.

"Are you new?" I asked, trying to be friendly
because I felt so sorry for her.

"Aren't we all?"

"I meant new in the neighborhood."

"No," she said, puzzled. "I went to Parkside."

"Oh, well, that's why I don't know you." I
felt a little embarrassed. I hoped she hadn't
guessed that I thought she was new to the area—
the state, the *planet!*—because she looked so weird.

"I'm Tamara Cherp," she said.

I felt myself on the verge of giggling, of repeating, "Tamara *Cherp?*" and really hurting her
feelings. Then I saw two girls poke each other and
bite their lips to keep from laughing as they looked
sideways at her, and my heart went out to Tamara
Cherp.

"I'm Bonnie Snyder," I said. "How do you
like the place so far?"

Tamara Cherp shrugged. "Whether I like it
or not, the law says I have to be here till I'm six-
teen. So what difference does it make?"

"I never thought about it that way." And I didn't think I was going to like this girl very much, either. She seemed sort of sullen and antisocial.

So I was surprised—to say the least—when Spanish was over and Tamara invited me to come home with her.

"Well, I don't know. See, I have to take the bus, and it's the first day and all, and I'm not sure—"

"Okay." Tamara shrugged. "No big deal."

I wondered if it was hard for her to make friends, and how many times she'd tried and been rejected. Maybe it had happened so often she *expected* me to say no. Saying "no big deal" was just a cover-up, so I wouldn't see how hurt she was by this newest rejection.

"No, hey, listen, I *want* to, I just thought I'd better take my own bus the first day, so I know how to get home. I could come tomorrow if you want."

"Okay. I walk. It's only a few blocks from here. My mother can drive you home."

"Fine. See you tomorrow."

· ·

By the next afternoon, I was sorry I'd ever felt sorry for Tamara Cherp. A whole bunch of my old friends were going to the mall and they'd asked me to meet them. Now I couldn't. Not only that, I was beginning to talk to people in my classes, beginning to realize I would make new friends in high school. I didn't even *like* Tamara Cherp. I didn't particularly want to be friends with her. Why should I feel guilty because she'd been rejected by other people?

But there was nothing I could do about it without feeling more guilty. I'd agreed to go to her house, and I'd go—just this once. That didn't mean I'd have to be bosom buddies with her. It might be a little uncomfortable sitting next to her in Spanish all year if she kept hitting me with invitations, but I couldn't help that.

On the four-block walk to Tamara's house, we hardly exchanged four words. I didn't think I'd have to worry about her getting too friendly. We didn't seem to have anything to say to each other.

Tamara opened the door to her house, which was unlocked—a foolish thing, I thought, even in our quiet neighborhood—and we walked into the living room.

In the middle of the floor, someone dressed in a purple leotard and lots of bead necklaces was standing on her head. I couldn't see her face, because the beads dangled down over it and covered it almost completely.

"Hi, Cerise. This is Bonnie."

Cerise must be her sister. She lowered her knees to the floor slowly and came up out of her headstand.

"This is my mother, Cerise," Tamara said.

I was surprised that Tamara called her mother by her first name—not to mention surprised at the name—but then Cerise pulled on a long red-and-yellow skirt and threw a fringed shawl over her purple shoulders, and all I could think of was: So this is where Tamara gets her taste in clothes!

"Hi, Bonnie," Cerise said. She walked over to me and held out her hand. I shook it. "Welcome to our house."

"Thank you. That was a terrific headstand. I've been trying for years, but I always fall over."

"It takes preparation and practice," Cerise said. "But it's worth the effort. It gets the blood rushing to the brain, starts the creative juices flowing, gives you mental energy, and it's super for sinus trouble."

"Have you got sinus trouble?"

"No, but I can use all the creative juices I can stir up. I'm going nuts trying to come up with new slogans."

"New slogans? For what? Are you in advertising?"

Cerise grinned broadly. Her whole face lit up

when she smiled, and I realized she looked young enough to actually be Tamara's sister.

"Not exactly. Not the kind you mean. Come on in the kitchen, I'll show you."

I heard Tamara give a deep sigh. I glanced over at her. She looked bored.

We followed Cerise into the kitchen. There were picket signs everywhere. The materials for picket signs littered the floor and the kitchen table. The signs were stacked in corners, against the side of the refrigerator, leaning against the walls.

"Did you do all these yourself?" I asked.

"No, we've been working on them for a week. A whole committee of us. But the demonstration is this Saturday, and we don't have enough yet, and everyone had something else to do today, so I got stuck finishing up. And I'm sick of painting 'No Nukes' and 'Save Our Land' over and over again."

"How about 'No Nukes Is Good Nukes'?" I blurted out, without even thinking.

Cerise gave a little shriek of delight. "That's fan*ta*stic! Tamara, where did you find this *pearl?*"

Tamara looked as if she'd like to toss this pearl back to the oyster.

"Spanish," she said.

" 'No Nukes Is Good Nukes,' " Cerise mused. "I *love* it!"

"If you need some help," I said tentatively, "we could do some signs for you. I'm not great at lettering, but—"

"Oh, no," Cerise protested. "You didn't come here to paint picket signs. I can't impose on you like that. Even if everybody *did* fink out on me, I'm sure you and Tamara—"

"I don't mind," I said. "Really. It'd be fun. Wouldn't it, Tamara?"

Tamara scowled. I didn't think she thought it would be fun. But I did. A lot more fun than talking to—or not talking to—Tamara. Except for the clothes, it was hard to believe she was Cerise's daughter. Cerise was so lively and cheerful, so involved and friendly. Tamara acted sulky and aloof.

"I suppose," Tamara said sourly, "this means the Colonel is cooking dinner again tonight?"

"Now, Tamara, it's only a couple of days till the demonstration, and then we'll be able to get to the stove again. By Monday everything will be back to normal."

Tamara snorted. She muttered something under her breath. It sounded like, "Till next month."

It was a great afternoon. Cerise told us about the hideous things that could happen if there was an accident at a nuclear power plant and read us excerpts from secret hearings held after a near disaster at the site they were going to picket.

Tamara yawned a lot. I guess she must have heard all this stuff before but I hadn't, and I was fascinated. It was as scary as a good horror movie. And Cerise was so enthusiastic about my sign-painting and my slogan, she made me feel like the demonstration couldn't take place without my help.

Cerise drove me home. Tamara sat in the backseat of the Volkswagen and didn't say a word except "good-bye" as I got out in my driveway.

"You must come again," Cerise said warmly. "It was a joy meeting you. And thanks for all your help."

"It was fun." I glanced at Tamara. I didn't think she'd be too eager to have me come again. But then, that was okay. I hadn't planned on visiting her again. I just went today because I'd promised. I didn't want to be friends with Tamara.

But what a shame I couldn't be friends with Cerise.

I went into my house. My mother was sitting in the living room working on a needlepoint picture of a country church.

"Hi, Janet," I said experimentally.

She looked up, startled. "Hi *Janet?* What happened to Mom?"

"You don't mind if I call you Janet, do you?"

"Actually, I do. I waited a long time to be

called Mom, and you're the only person who can call me that."

"Oh, *Mother*."

"Of course, when you say it like that, I have second thoughts."

"It's just that if I call you Janet we're more like equals. We can relate to each other on a person-to-person basis, instead of—"

"What makes you think we're equals?" my mother asked, dropping her needlepoint.

"Wouldn't it be nice if we were more like friends than mother and daughter?"

"I *have* friends," my mother said. "I want a daughter."

"You know, you're awfully old-fashioned," I said in exasperation.

"I know," she replied comfortably, and picked up her needlepoint.

....

Surprisingly enough, a couple of weeks later Tamara invited me to her house again. I got the definite impression that she only asked me because Cerise pushed her into it. Although Tamara and I still didn't have very much to say to each other, and I still didn't want to be friends with her, I couldn't help but feel flattered that Cerise liked me enough to want me to come over.

I couldn't tell whether Tamara was pleased or resentful when I said I would. I think Tamara guessed it was Cerise I really wanted to visit.

When we got to the house, Cerise was in the kitchen. She heard the door open and called out to us. "Tamara? Did Bonnie come?"

Hearing the eagerness in Cerise's voice, I felt a warm glow. Even Tamara's almost sarcastic, "Yes, Bonnie came," didn't diminish my pleasure.

"Come say hello," Cerise yelled. "I can't move. I'm up to my elbows in tofu."

Tamara rolled her eyes toward the ceiling. She trudged into the kitchen. I followed, wondering what tofu was, and how someone up to their elbows in it would look.

Cerise was standing next to the sink, working at a wooden chopping block. The kitchen table was littered with papers, books, a typewriter, pencils, and a sketch pad. The kitchen counter was chaos— bottles, jars, cans, utensils. It looked like an earthquake in a supermarket.

"Bonnie!" Cerise cried. "It's good to see you again. Can you stay for dinner?"

"Think twice before you answer that," Tamara said.

"Oh, Tamara, don't be so negative. Tonight I think I've really outdone myself. This is going to be my *pièce de résistance*."

"What are you making?" I asked curiously. It must be something pretty spectacular, I thought, considering the mess in the kitchen.

"Something with tofu in it," Tamara said.

"Well, of course, dear. I still have twenty recipes to go."

"Recipes for what?" I asked.

"My cookbook. *One Hundred and One Things To Do with Tofu.*"

"I can think of a hundred and second," Tamara said grimly.

"You're writing a cookbook?" I said. "Hey, that's great. But what's tofu?"

"Bean curd. And it's fantastic. It has tons of protein! I mean, you wouldn't believe, ounce for ounce, the nourishment you can get out of tofu compared to meat. And the cost is so much less."

She was cutting some white stuff into cubes.

"Is that it?" I asked.

"Yes. Want to try some?"

"I don't know. It looks kind of—"

"I know. Bland. It is, really. That's why you have to be ingenious using it. But it's incredibly versatile. I've come up with some marvelous dishes. This is going to be a tofu and broccoli casserole *gratinée.*"

For a second Tamara looked almost faint. She actually turned pale.

Cerise finished up the casserole and popped it into the oven. I offered to help her clean the kitchen, and the next thing I knew, Tamara and I were standing over the sink and Cerise was sitting at the table, sipping a cup of Red Zinger tea and reading us excerpts from her cookbook.

Tamara's face was like a thundercloud.

Well, what did she expect? I wondered. She didn't invite me because she wanted to. She invited me because Cerise asked her to.

I didn't stay for dinner. It wasn't the tofu. I tasted it, and I could see how you could do an awful lot with it to make it interesting. Plain, it tasted like custard without any sugar in it, but I was sure Cerise had wonderful ways to cook it. I just have this thing about broccoli. I told Cerise I was allergic.

When I got home, my mother was in the kitchen.

"What's for dinner?" I asked.

"Roast beef, Yorkshire pudding, spinach and bacon salad, and broiled tomatoes."

"Boring," I muttered. "Boring."

She stared at me as if I were crazy.

"Do you realize that for the price of that roast beef you could have bought ten pounds of tofu?"

"No, I didn't realize that. And I don't think I care for tofu all that much. Oh, it's nice to find a little piece of it in my soup at a Japanese restaurant, but that's about it. I can't conceive of ten pounds of tofu."

"You're not very adventurous, you know that?" I said.

"You've forgotten my asparagus and squid salad," she said sweetly.

••••••••••••••••••••••••

Every few weeks Tamara would ask me over to her house, and I would go. We talked a little more now, but not about anything personal, except Cerise. Tamara really didn't appreciate her mother.

Cerise was always involved in something interesting. One time it was organizing a crafts fair to raise funds for an American Indian museum. (Only Cerise called them Native Americans, not Indians.)

Tamara said the reason Cerise wanted to have a crafts fair was because she had just gotten a potter's wheel and was now into pottery, and she thought it would be a good way to display her own crafts. I thought that was pretty nasty of Tamara, but I wasn't surprised. Tamara just didn't have any sense of perspective where her mother was concerned.

Another time Cerise was taking a course in Chinese and was totally immersed, not only in the language, but also in the history and culture of

China. She was hoping to take a trip to China within a year, and she wanted to be prepared to get the most out of it when she went.

"I don't want to be just another tourist snapping pictures of everything," Cerise said scornfully. "When I go, I want to *feel* Chinese, *think* Chinese, *understand* Chinese, *live* Chinese. You have to prepare for that kind of experience."

I hoped that part of the preparation would be *eating* Chinese, but unfortunately, Cerise wasn't into *cooking* Chinese. She just didn't have the time. She got some stuff from McDonald's.

Tamara would visit her father when Cerise went to China. Tamara's father lived in California, and she saw him summers. I wondered, being divorced and all, why Cerise didn't have to work. Unless Tamara's father was very rich and sent them piles of money, how did they manage?

I sort of hinted around the subject one day, saying something like, with all Cerise's projects, it was a good thing she didn't have to work, or she'd never have time for the really important things in life.

Tamara almost smiled. "Even without working," she said, "she doesn't have time for them."

I didn't know what she meant. Tamara saw my puzzled look and then really did smile. But it was a strange smile.

"You know, I've never met *your* mother, Bonnie."

"Hey, that's right," I said, trying to sound as if I just realized it. I hadn't, of course, just realized it, but I'd been avoiding inviting Tamara to my house. The only reason I went to *her* house was to visit with Cerise; if I invited Tamara to my house, she might take it as a sign I wanted to be friendlier.

But I couldn't be rude forever. Or pretend not to be aware that I'd been at Tamara's eight times, and she'd been at my house zero.

"How about tomorrow?" I asked.

. . . .

"Nice," Tamara said, coming into the living room. "Comfortable."

"I guess," I said, sort of startled. "I never thought about it. It's boring, though. Not like your house. There's always something interesting—"

My mother called out hello from the kitchen.

We went in and I introduced Tamara.

Tamara just stood there and stared at my mother. My mother stared back. Tamara looked particularly bizarre today in purple harem pants, a bright green shirt, and a rope of beads that hung down to her waist.

My mother was clipping coupons out of the newspaper, making separate little piles of them on the table.

I looked at one of the coupons. It was for dog food.

"We don't have a dog," I said.

"The Jarmans do."

"You just like cutting out things," I said.

"Everybody needs a hobby."

I was mortified. Tamara gazed at my mother, the mad coupon-clipper, and I knew she must be comparing her to Cerise, who had more important, more interesting, more intelligent things to do with her time than to cut out coupons for things she didn't need. Right now Cerise was probably saving the whale, or standing on her head, or studying arc welding by mail.

It was hard to believe that up to two years ago my mother had had a responsible job. When she decided to quit, she said she'd worked for fifteen years, and she'd probably work again in a couple of years, but right then she wanted to *rest*. My father was making enough money so we wouldn't starve, and if she found she was going crazy just sitting home, she'd go back to work.

But she hadn't gone crazy.

She enjoyed it. All she did was read, do

needlepoint, shop, cook, clean the house, and work in the garden. And, of course, clip coupons.

I didn't understand it at all.

"That's not really her hobby," I said. "She just does it to save money."

"What's wrong with that?" my mother asked. "Stop apologizing for me and take something to eat. You must be hungry."

We got some potato chips and Cokes. I figured I'd have to ask Tamara up to my room, and we'd have to try to make some conversation for a while, but just then my mother glanced up at the clock.

"Three-thirty! I'm missing *Doctor's Hospital*!"

This was really embarrassing. Why did the only soap opera she watched have to be on now, when Tamara could see her practically leaping out of her chair and sprinting into the family room to turn the TV on? She'd think my mother spent her whole day watching those dumb shows.

"You like that, too?" Tamara said. "Hey, would it be all right if I watched with you? I hate to miss it. I can't wait to see what happens when Brick finds out Blake is his real father."

"You watch that drivel?" I said incredulously. But I said it to Tamara's back. She was already headed for the family room with her Coke.

"Sure, come on. It's just starting."

My mother patted the couch next to her, and Tamara sat down.

"Come on, Bonnie," my mother said. "It won't kill you to watch it just this once."

I couldn't believe it. I trudged into the family room, plopped down on a chair with my Coke and the potato chips, and sat there for an hour, bored out of my mind.

But what else could I do? All those times I'd been at Tamara's house, she'd stayed with me, no matter what Cerise and I were doing. I couldn't just walk out of the room, bored or not. Maybe all the afternoons I'd spent at her house painting signs, cleaning up tofu, and learning to say *cloud* in Mandarin Chinese, Tamara had really wanted to be watching her soap opera but felt she had to stay with her guest.

Maybe, I thought, remembering the look of impatience I'd seen so often on her face, maybe Tamara was just as bored with all those things as I was sitting there watching *Doctor's Hospital.*

During the commercials, they compared their favorite characters on the show and argued amiably about whether Noelle really had amnesia or was faking it to get out of testifying at Buck's trial.

I couldn't believe it. How could Tamara, daughter of the most fascinating, active, youthful mother I'd ever seen, be sitting here with *my* mother, staring at the boob tube as if it were as important as, say, nuclear disaster?

When the program was over, Tamara and I went up to my room.

"She's really nice, your mother," Tamara said.

"Well, yeah. But she must seem awfully . . . ordinary . . . compared to Cerise."

"Sometimes ordinariness is a relief," Tamara said softly.

"Want to trade?" I joked.

"Would you want to?" Tamara asked. "I mean, think about it. Would you really?"

··························

I thought about it. Long after Tamara left, I was still thinking about it. Would I want Cerise for my mother, instead of my own mother? It was exciting to visit Tamara's house: There was always something interesting going on. Cerise was always on a new kick, busy, involved, full of vitality.

But, I realized, none of those things had anything to do with Tamara. Cerise didn't seem to be all that involved in Tamara's activities—whatever they were—and Tamara wasn't interested in Cerise's projects.

But I would be, I told myself. I'd enjoyed painting picket signs, helping Cerise with her cookbook, learning how to say *cloud* in Chinese.

But that was as a visitor. Maybe living with Cerise was different than dropping in once a month.

She's like New York, I thought suddenly. Cerise is like that cliché about New York. "It's a great place to visit, but I wouldn't want to live there."

How strange. I hadn't thought about my mother like this before. In fact, I hadn't given all that much thought to my mother for years.

I walked downstairs into the kitchen. My mother was stir-frying something at the stove.

"You know what, Mom? You're a lot like Bent Fork, Tennessee."

She looked up from her wok. *"What?"*

I put my arm around her. "It's a compliment. Believe me. I hope you never change."

"Oh, honey, what a nice thing to say." She positively beamed.

"What's for dinner? Smells delicious."

"I hope you like it. You inspired me. It's tofu and bean sprouts. Bonnie! Bonnie, what's the matter? You look so pale."

I Hate You,
Wallace B. Pokras

I hate you, Wallace B. Pokras.

After all we've meant to each other, how could you do this to me?

Maybe I was wrong. Maybe we haven't meant that much to each other. Maybe you were just hanging around with me till Ms. Right came along.

Using me, that's what you were doing. Just using me as a convenient date: someone to go to dances with, someone to take to team parties, someone handy for social occasions.

Handy. Like a pocket calculator. And you *did* have me in the palm of your hand, didn't you? What a dope I was.

I mean, I really thought those kisses meant something to you. I thought they were sincere kisses. I would never kiss someone I didn't love— or at the very least, like a whole lot.

But they lied, Wallace, you worm. Those kisses lied. You have lying lips. They go perfectly with your cheating heart.

A regular Benedict Arnold, that's what you are. A traitor, a fink, a creep, a . . .

You think I didn't see you. I'll bet you thought you could get away with it. How were you to know I'd be at the movies last night? And how were you to know that at the last minute I'd decided to go with Pam and Becky because you told me you'd be busy?

Busy. Boy, you were busy all right. Busy as a little beaver.

Well, you've got a surprise coming, Wallace. You didn't get away with it. I saw you. I saw you with that blonde—that refugee from a jeans commercial. It was dark and the movie had already started, but I saw you walk down the aisle with her looking for seats in the front. You're not hard to spot, you know, you big hunk. *I mean hulk!* Hulk is what I meant. Even with the lights down, your hair still looks like it's on fire. Even when you slouch, you're still practically six feet tall.

You looked ridiculous with her, you know. She was barely five feet tall. You look like Mutt and Jeff together. I never did get to see her face. I was so humiliated I dragged Pam and Becky out of the movies while the final credits were still rolling. So all I saw were your backs as you walked toward some empty seats. I don't know how she managed to sit down at all in those jeans. They looked like they were painted on with a spray can.

Yes, you have a real surprise coming, Wallace Benedict Arnold Pokras. Because I'm just going to sit here by the phone, waiting for you to call.

Oh, you'll call. Eventually. You'll have to. Either to try and pretend nothing ever happened, while you're planning to keep both of us on the string at the same time or to make some lame excuse about why we can't go to Jerry's party next Saturday.

So I'm just going to sit here by the phone and wait.

And when you call, you're going to get it right between the eyes.

They hanged Benedict Arnold, you know. (Or did they shoot him? I'm not sure.) Whichever, it's too good for you. Too quick. Too easy.

You're going to suffer, Wallace, like you're making me suffer. A long, slow, agonizing revenge, that's what I'm going to give you.

Ever read "The Pit and the Pendulum," Wallace?

We had to read it for English this year. Which means you had to read it last year but probably didn't. You'd be failing again right now if it weren't for me, Wallace. You ungrateful rat!

Or is that why you started going with me? Because I'm good in English? You really *are* using me! You have to pass English to stay on the team. And the minute football season is over, you're going to drop me like an old shoe.

Oh, Wallace, you calculating, scheming, conniving, lying . . .

Well, there are still three weeks left in the football season. Let's see you pull through your English midterm without me. Because if you think you can expect any help from me, you've got another think coming.

And after I gave you the best months of my life.

What I don't understand is why you spent the whole summer with me. You didn't need me then. You didn't even have to go to summer school after I tutored you for two weeks before finals, and got you through English 11 by the skin of your teeth.

Was it gratitude?

Hah! You haven't got a grateful bone in your oversized body. If you had, you wouldn't be sneaking around darkened movie theaters with that bargain basement Brooke Shields.

Letting you fail English and watching you get kicked off the team is a start; a good start, true, but just a start. You're going to have to suffer a lot more than that before justice is done.

I'm not a vindictive person, Wallace. Not normally. I'm not mean or spiteful. Even when Pam grabbed the very last suede fringed vest on sale at Zohlmann's for a ridiculously low price right out from under my nose, I didn't bear a grudge. She got it first; her hand was faster, and even though it was *me* who said, "Oh, look at that fantastic vest!" I was a good sport about it. Even though it was too big for her and would have been absolutely *perfect* for me, I didn't brood over it.

Fair's fair, she grabbed it first, though there'll probably *never* be a sale like that again, and that vest was *exactly* the thing I needed to wear with my new antelope cords, and the one time I asked to borrow it she *said* it was at the cleaners.

I'm just not the type to harp on something like that.

But love is not a suede vest, Wallace, you louse.

Or what I thought was love. What you let me believe was love. Or what you led me to believe was love. Or at the very least, like. With demonstrations of affection. Holding my hand at the shopping mall; dunking me in the pool; hugging me when I beat you three times in a row at Pac-Man; kissing me under the porch light, not caring that Jerry and Becky were sitting in the car ogling us.

Being betrayed by someone with whom you thought you had a deep and meaningful relationship brings out the dark, ugly side of a person's nature, Wallace. It leads a person to think—and do—things she would never ever consider under ordinary circumstances, particularly if she is of such a calm, understanding, unspiteful nature as I am.

Things like slipping rat poison into your Gatorade. (How appropriate, Wallace. Rat poison for a rat.) Or driving a stake through your heart. Or telling your new little playmate that you're deranged, and while you look like a normal person, every time there's a full moon you develop an unholy craving for chicken hearts.

But those are all too easy, Wallace, you crumb. (Except for that last one, which isn't bad.) No, whatever my revenge is, it has to be slow, drawn-out: fitting punishment for your betrayal.

Something like this: On the day of the big game with Northside, the game that decides the Section II Championship, you "accidentally" fall down the stairs and sprain your ankle. Nothing big and serious, you understand. Just a dumb old sprained ankle. It's such a stupid, careless injury. But you won't be able to put any weight on your foot, so you'll sit on the bench the whole time and watch as Northside wipes the field with us, because you're not in there to stop them on defense.

And you'll watch as the first quarter goes by, then the second and the third, and Northside will be rolling up points, because you're the star defensive back and everyone depends on you.

And the fourth quarter will drag by and everyone will know that if it weren't for you and your stupid ankle, Jefferson would have won the game, the section championship, and gone on to the county finals.

And when the game is over and you feel lower than a worm (which is what you are, anyway) and everyone's trying not to hate you—or at least, trying not to show that they hate you—I'll come up to you and say, "Oh, Wallace, what a shame. I guess you didn't know there was a scout from Ohio State here to watch you today . . ."

Mean? Rotten? Nasty? Sadistic?

You bet. But only what you deserve, Wallace. How do you think *I* feel right now? Right this minute? Sitting here by the phone, waiting for you to call, but dreading it at the same time. Wanting you to be able to explain everything but knowing you can't, knowing it's over, that what we once had is forever shattered, like a mirror broken into a hundred unlucky pieces.

I remember the first day we met. The guidance office told me they had someone who needed tutoring in English, and there you were, your hair looking like it was on fire, this great, big hunk— I mean *hulk!* Hulk is what I mean—looking like a nursery-school kid who'd flunked fingerpainting.

"I feel kind of stupid having a tutor who's younger than me," you said. You looked down at your great, big feet, hoping, I suppose, that I wouldn't notice your face turning the same color as your hair.

"Barbara is an honor student," Mrs. Rizzo had said. "She can give you help in the basics, which is really what you need."

"Barbie," you said. "Like the doll."

"Hardly," I said coolly, thinking, Boy, this one's a real nerd.

But you didn't turn out to be a nerd, Wallace.

A rat, a louse, a fink, a creep, a crumb, a Benedict Arnold, yes. But not a nerd.

I thought you were nice.

Gentle.

Honest.

Decent.

Even though I thought at first you were illiterate, you liked it when I read poetry to you. You said it was so romantic.

That's a great gimmick, Wallace. Go all misty-eyed when your tutor reads "How do I love thee?" Take her hand and whisper, "I'd like to learn that one by heart so I could say it to you." And blush. That was a really nice touch, that shy, embarrassed blush.

And it was all an act? Are you that good an actor? Were you stringing me along right from the beginning? Were you telling all the guys, "She really fell for me. She's going to put her heart and soul into *this* tutoring job. Don't worry about my eligibility next year."

How could you be so sly, so devious, so dishonest? How could you toss my heart around like a football, trifle with my affections, trample my dreams into shreds with your cleats?

Maybe two can playact at this game, Wallace, you con man.

Maybe when you do call, I won't let on that I saw you with that bleached blonde in her sprayed-on jeans. Oh, I could tell her hair was bleached, even though it was dark in the theater and I could only see her from the back, so I couldn't really check for black roots. No one is born with hair the color of Kraft Vanilla Caramels. That's probably not the only phony thing about her either. I'll bet that man-eating little shrimp is 99 and 44/100 percent artificial ingredients.

But maybe I won't say a word about her. Maybe I'll just act as if absolutely nothing has happened. Everything's fine. Everything's just dandy. I'll pretend that nothing has changed between us. We'll go on just as before.

And then I'll start tutoring you for your English midterm.

And I'll teach you all the wrong answers.

I'll tell you that Charles Dickens wrote *Catcher in the Rye* to expose the evils of the bread industry in Victorian England. I'll tell you that the past tense of sneak is snuck. I'll tell you that alliteration means the art of writing letters. I'll tell you that *The Rubaiyat of Omar Khayyam* is a poem about a rich guy with a yacht entirely encrusted with rubies.

And then, when you flunk your English midterm and get kicked off the team, you'll come to me and say, "But I wrote the answers you gave me! You *told* me that poem was about a guy with a red boat."

And I'll say, "And you told me you loved me." (Practically.) "Betrayal for betrayal, Wallace. Let the punishment fit the crime. By the way, in case anyone asks you, that's from a song by Stephen Foster. How does it feel, Wallace, to be betrayed by someone you trusted?"

And then he'd realize that I'd known all along. That I'd been acting, just as he'd been acting, that I hadn't been fooled.

"Time to pay the piper, Wallace. As in *The Pied Piper of Hamelin,* by Edna St. Vincent Millay. How does it feel?"

Sweet revenge. Mean, rotten, nasty, sadistic, devious . . .

But I'll never pull it off.

I hate you, Wallace B. Pokras. And I'll never be able to hide it for three weeks while I pretend to still love you. I don't even know if I'll be able to speak to you and sound normal when that phone rings, let alone deceive you for three weeks the way you've deceived me all these months.

It's just not like me, Wallace. Spitefulness, meanness of spirit, vindictive acts of violence simply aren't in my nature. That's why it's so hard for me to think up exactly the right mean, rotten, nasty, sadistic thing to do to you.

But give me time. I'll overcome my basic decency and think of something that will make you sorry you were ever—

The phone.

My hand is shaking.

"Hello?" My voice is shaking, too. I hope he doesn't notice. If it's him.

It's him.

"Your cousin Ginger from Baltimore? To the Empire State Building? . . . That's where you were all day? Oh, Wallace! . . . Crying? No, of course not. I think I'm getting a little cold, that's all. . . . Tonight? You mean, with Ginger and your aunt and uncle? . . . Oh, yes! I mean, I'd love to. . . . No, I'm sure my brother would just love to meet Ginger. . . . She's *twelve?* . . . Yeah, perfect. . . . Last night? . . . You *were?* . . . Isn't that the funniest coincidence. So was I! For goodness sake, you must have walked right by me and I never saw you. . . ."

The Girl
Who Had
Everything

*T*his really happened, though it's so crazy that even the people who saw it aren't sure they believe it, either.

I suppose it probably started way back in fifth grade, when Warren Schultz bought Diane a fake ruby ring from Woolworth's and, in front of a whole circle of our giggling classmates, asked her, very solemnly, to marry him.

That was the thing about Diane. Even in the fifth grade, when the boys either treat girls like zoo animals or friends of no particular sex, it was different for her. She had something—I'm not sure what it was—that drove normally shy, awkward, or downright boorish ten- and eleven-year-old boys to make utter fools of themselves over her.

Anyway, she looked at that ring, and she looked at Warren, who was four inches shorter than she was and skinny as a stick, and said thoughtfully, "I can't promise to marry you, Warren, but we could be engaged if you want."

Everybody clapped and cheered, Warren

beamed, and Diane slipped the ring on her finger and held her hand out to see how it looked. I don't think she said two words to Warren after that day, but she wore the ring for months.

To say Diane had "something" is putting it mildly. Diane had *everything*. I didn't realize it till we were older and I became more aware of the differences between us, but by that time we'd been friends for so long that I guess we stayed friends out of habit, rather than because of common interests.

She wasn't beautiful, not in the movie-star sense, but, like Scarlett O'Hara, somehow she made you think she was. She had dark auburn hair and hazel eyes, which changed color depending on what she was wearing. Something happened to a boy when he looked into those eyes. In school we read about Medusa, who turned men into stone if they looked at her. Diane turned them into Jell-O.

She was an only child, and her parents thought she was the greatest thing since sliced bread. Her mother never just talked about Diane. It was always *our* Diane. Her father called her his "little princess." I was very impressed with that, especially when we were young. I once asked my father why he never called me his little princess, and he looked at me like I was crazy and said, "We come from a long line of commoners."

So I guess even then I sensed there was something about Diane that made her different from all us commoners. Somebody who grows up being called "Princess" probably acquires a certain aura that someone who grows up being called "Hon" simply never achieves.

It goes without saying that Diane got whatever her heart desired. It didn't hurt that her parents had plenty of money, but you knew that even if they didn't they would have somehow managed to provide their Diane with whatever it was she thought she wanted, the instant she wanted it.

Spoiled? Well, I guess so, in the sense that Diane was used to getting her own way, used to getting whatever she wanted, and probably expected that Life would continue to provide her with everything, just as her parents always had.

Although, in fifth and sixth grades, the boys were Diane-crazy, Diane did not turn boy-crazy until the beginning of the seventh grade. Until then she'd been content to sort of drift along, taking it for granted that boys would trip over each other trying to sit behind her on the school bus (I always sat next to her) or stage shoving matches in the auditorium as long as the seat on the other side of Diane was empty (which was never long) or use their lunch money to buy her candy bars.

You or I might have gotten pimples from all

those candy bars, but not Diane. Her skin was like the weather forecast for heaven: eternally fair and clear. Zits were simply not in Diane's destiny.

Anyway, as I said, Diane remained pretty nonchalant about all this male attention until we hit seventh grade. Then, wham! Diane fell in love.

Diane fell in love with Arthur Dotson.

And Richard Weaver.

And Bobby Schwartz.

And Dennis Taliaferro.

And David Gordon.

And Alan DeMarco.

Not all at once, of course, although—being Diane—she probably could have handled that, too. But first was Arthur Dotson. He sat next to her in English. She agonized a full half hour one afternoon over whether he would like her back. The following day she sat down next to him, turned the full force of her hazel eyes on him, and murmured, "Oh, Arthur, I don't have a pen."

Arthur gave her his Cross pen. To keep. That may have been the very moment when Diane realized that no male alive could resist the power of those hazel eyes.

In any case, she went with Arthur for three weeks. She was the first girl I knew who actually "went" with anybody.

"What does it mean when you go with someone?" I asked her one day. "What do you have to do?"

"Oh, nothing much," she said. "You just hang out together. You know."

"Do you have to let him kiss you?"

"Of course. We're not babies anymore, you know."

"Do you like it?"

Diane shrugged. "It's okay."

If Diane was less than thrilled with Arthur's kisses, his presents made up for it. Now that we were in junior high, we'd passed the candy bar stage, and Arthur's gifts were pretty neat, I thought. A great big stuffed Snoopy, which Diane kept on her bed; a ten karat gold-filled locket in the shape of a heart; and a license plate for her bike, with DIANE stamped on it in big, red letters.

Not to mention the Cross pen, which Diane said didn't count.

But after three weeks, Diane got tired of Arthur and fell in love with Richard Weaver. He was no more immune to the hazel eyes than Arthur. And he was no slouch with presents either.

And so it went, all through junior high school. Diane loved them and left them. I don't know if they were any wiser when she was finished with them, but they certainly were sadder.

She switched boyfriends on the average of

every three to six weeks. I told her it must be all the TV she watched.

"What do you mean?"

"Haven't you read those studies where they found that kids have watched about forty-six thousand hours of television by the time they get to be our age?"

"So what?"

"All that television watching makes for a very short attention span."

"I don't know what you're talking about."

"You get tired of your boyfriends so fast," I said. "Do you think that's the way it's supposed to be?"

Diane looked at me, her eyes wide with surprise. "Well, of course! Imagine if they got tired of *me* first!"

When we hit high school Diane, as you'd expect, made a big splash, while I sort of stood at the shoreline, testing the temperature of the water with my toe.

Considering how fickle she was, you'd think Diane would have been tired of me by now, particularly since being popular took an enormous amount of her time. Why, cheerleading alone—of course she made cheerleaders; did you doubt for a moment that she would?—required hours and hours every week, especially during basketball season. And it wasn't just cheerleading. There were plays to star in, clubs to preside over, student government to run. So what did she need *me* for?

To talk to.

Diane was a wonderful talker, an inspired talker, a nonstop talker. True, she talked almost exclusively about herself, but then, what more fascinating topic was there?

Watching her talk to a boy was like attending a clinic in conversation. She could make a trip to the dentist, studying for a geometry test, or a failed attempt at baking cookies episodes of such high dramatic impact that her listener hung on every word, leaning forward eagerly, mouth slightly open in wonder, eyes fixed longingly on hers. He was, in the traditional, fairy-tale sense of the word, enchanted.

But she talked to me differently than she talked to boys, and that was why she needed me. The subject of the conversation was the same, naturally—herself—but the nature of it was different. I was there to hear things she couldn't tell anyone else, to listen to her troubles, to help calm her fears, to allay her self-doubts.

You think Diane didn't have any troubles? You think she had no fears, never lost her confidence? Well, you might be right. But *she* thought she did, and that's what counts.

"I don't think Paul likes me anymore. Maybe I shouldn't have told him about sleeping with my Snoopy. I mean, I was just being funny, you know, but after all, he's a senior and maybe he thinks I'm juvenile now that he knows I sleep with a stuffed animal. And he hasn't called me since yesterday. I don't understand it. Just last Saturday he said my eyes were the mirrors of my soul, and they were so beautiful he knew my soul was beautiful, too. Isn't that the most beautiful thing you ever heard?"

"Beautiful," I agreed. Not original but beautiful.

"Now, how could he say that on Saturday and be tired of me by today? What will I do without Paul? He hasn't even said a word about the Senior Prom, and if he liked me you'd think he'd at least *mention* it."

"Diane, that's five months away. You'll probably be tired of Paul by then and be going with somebody else."

"Maybe *he's* tired of *me* right now. And how could you think I'd go with anyone else? Paul is all I want. Just watching him out there on the basketball field—"

"Court," I corrected.

"And seeing him score all those points and cheering for him and knowing he knows I'm doing those cartwheels just for him, like he's scoring all those points just for me—"

"And he looks so cute in his shorts," I said.

"Doesn't he? Oh, I couldn't bear to lose him."

"Especially not at the height of the basketball season."

"That's right," she said tearfully. "That would be awful. And you know, I'm really having trouble with my cartwheel. I don't know what's the matter with me. I just can't keep my back straight and I'm always landing bent over. I know I look terrible, and I'm making a fool of myself in front of the whole school. Do you think they'll kick me off cheerleaders for not being able to do the cartwheel right? I mean, even though I am head cheerleader, it's the first time they let anyone but a senior be head cheerleader, and maybe Ms. Jenkins will think they made a mistake. . . ."

And so on.

Somehow I never got tired of listening to Diane talk about Diane. Maybe it was because I was so much on the outside looking in. I would never actually *be* the girl who has everything, but through Diane, at least I got a taste of what it might be like.

Wasn't I jealous?

Well, yes, a little. It's hard not to envy someone who gets everything she wants, who never had a thing go wrong for her in her life, who doesn't know what the short end of the stick looks like, whose biggest problem is turning a perfect cartwheel.

But on the other hand, I didn't want the same things Diane wanted, so if I didn't get them, it was no great disappointment. And besides, Diane cared about me—as much as she was capable of caring about anybody. Sometimes—not often—we talked about me.

For instance: "Why don't we do something about your hair?"

Or: "Should I get Paul to fix you up with one of his friends for New Year's Eve?"

Or: "Did you ever think about wearing contact lenses? The soft ones are supposed to be terrific."

Diane's agonizing over Paul was short-lived. He called her barely an hour after our conversation about him, and they talked for an hour. At least, that's the way Diane told it. I assume that Diane talked for an hour, and Paul hung onto every word as eagerly as he held onto the phone.

Diane really was crazy about Paul. She went with him longer than she'd ever gone with any boy. I kept waiting for the symptoms of restlessness to appear, particularly when basketball season ended. After all, she'd dropped Tom Noonan when football season was over. Somehow, she said, the excitement had gone out of the relationship when he hung up his shoulder pads for the year.

But the symptoms never appeared. Diane, at last, had found someone who stretched her attention span past six weeks. She was, she declared, deeply and eternally in love.

One of the things that kept her that way, she said, was that Paul was very interesting. "He's a great conversationalist," she told me. "We just talk for hours. We never seem to run out of things to talk about."

What—I was dying to say—do you mean, *we?*

One Saturday night a friend of Paul's was giving a party, and Diane insisted that I come. She said it didn't matter if I came alone, but if I wanted she'd fix me up with one of Paul's friends.

"You'll have a good time, I promise. Come on, a party's just what you need. And you might meet someone interesting."

Diane and Paul picked me up the night of the party, along with Eric Shulman, who was my "date" for the evening. (Chosen by Paul because Eric was as shy as I was. Obviously we were perfect for each other. Which sounds reasonable on paper but actually meant that we spent most of the evening in silence because neither of us could think of a thing to say.)

Yet, as it turned out, Diane was right.

The party was just what I needed.

Everything was going along fine—for Diane—until about ten-thirty. Till then she'd been, as usual, the center of attention; the main attraction, surrounded by boys. Paul stayed pretty close for the first hour of the party, but that didn't stop a host of other male admirers from clustering around and listening to "Diane Goes to the Dentist and Gets Laughing Gas." Followed by "Diane's Nightmare of Being Smothered by a Bear." (She wakes up, shrieking, to find her Snoopy's ear in her mouth.)

"You sleep with a stuffed dog?" one of the boys teased.

"Well, for heaven's sake," Diane said innocently, "I'm too young to sleep with anything else."

At ten-thirty, Diane had to go to the bathroom. She didn't really have to; she just wanted to check herself out, make sure that all the talking and eating hadn't left her face ravaged.

She took me with her.

"You and Eric seem to be getting along great," she said. Which just goes to show you how much attention she was paying to us.

" 'Me and Eric' haven't said two sentences to each other."

"Well, if he's shy it's up to you to get the old conversational ball rolling. Don't just stand there like a stick. Most boys are so shy they're relieved if a girl does all the talking. It sort of takes the pressure off them."

This piece of advice out of the way, Diane concentrated on her lipstick and hair and suggested I do the same. It was hardly urgent. Since we'd arrived at the party I'd barely moved my lips at all and had not once tossed my head back gaily as I laughed at my own wit.

When we got back to the party, Diane started to walk toward the spot where she'd left Paul. Suddenly she stopped short and looked around, puzzled.

"Where is he? He was right here."

"Maybe he went to the bathroom."

"But we were *in* the bathroom. He wasn't there."

"Maybe there's another bathroom."

Then Diane's fingers dug into my arm and I heard a little gasp. "Look!"

I looked.

Paul was sitting on the floor, opposite a girl with mousy brown hair and rimless glasses. She was plucking idly at a zither, but her eyes were intent on Diane's boyfriend. He was talking, gesturing with his hands, leaning over so their heads were practically touching, as if he were trying to emphasize certain Important Points.

Every once in a while she'd nod or smile or tilt her head questioningly. But as far as I could tell, she hardly said a word.

"What is he *doing?*" Diane hissed.

"He's just talking, Diane."

"But to *her?* Miranda Hull? *Why?*"

"Maybe he likes zither music. You know what they say."

"About what?"

"About music hathing charms to soothe the savage breast."

"But she's not playing anything. I mean, she's just sitting there like a lump. And she's such a nothing."

"Then there's nothing to worry about. Diane, *you* talk to other boys. Why are you making such a big deal—"

"That's different!" Diane said.

And she was right. It was.

Diane plopped down on the floor next to Paul and said, "Goodness, I thought you'd disappeared. I looked all over for you and I thought, Is it possible that a person can vanish into thin air just like that?" She put her hand on his arm and turned those hypnotic hazel eyes on him. Tonight they were a gorgeous liquid green, reflecting her angora sweater. "But you were here all the time, just talking to good old Miranda."

Paul looked briefly at Diane and let her eyes hold his for a moment. Then he said, "Right," and turned back to good old Miranda.

Paul drove us home—Diane, Eric, and me, *and* Miranda, who'd come alone and needed a lift. Since Miranda lived the farthest away, he dropped the rest of us off first.

I was sleeping over at Diane's. Eric and I bid each other a passionless farewell, and I followed Diane into the house, up to her room, and onto her bed, where she flung herself to have her tantrum.

"It's over, it's over! And for *her!* That *nothing!* That zither-playing zilch! Did you see how he humiliated me? In front of *everybody?*"

"Yes."

"I'll just die. I love him. You know I love him more than anyone I ever loved. I mean, I didn't even love any of the others. I just thought I did. I didn't know what true love was till Paul. How could he *do* this to me? How could he love me one minute and somebody else the next?"

"I don't know."

"Maybe he doesn't exactly love her. Not the way he loves me. That's impossible. It can't happen that fast. But he looked interested in her, didn't he? You certainly couldn't miss that. He definitely is interested in that—that nerd."

"Well . . ."

"He must have talked to her for two hours. *Two hours.* And did you see her? She just *sat* there. I mean, I don't think that girl said a word."

"Not very many, anyway."

"Then why? *Why?* What has she got? She's plain, she's mousy, she plays the *zither*, for heaven's sake. She doesn't know how to talk to boys—"

"Maybe she knows how to listen."

"What? Now, look, how could Paul go from a girl like me—I mean, in all modesty—from a girl like *me* to a girl like Miranda Hull? I just don't understand that."

"I know you don't," I said gently.

••••••••••••••••••••••

And neither did anybody else. It was all over school in three days. Diane was not exactly a non-entity in high school, and the fact that Paul had dropped her for Miranda Hull was Numero Uno on everyone's list of Choice Topics to Gossip About.

Because he *did* drop her. In a cowardly sort of way. He never actually came right out and said they were breaking off. He just never came right out and said *anything* to her after the party. He avoided her. Stopped calling.

Diane got the hint.

I don't know if she was more devastated by losing Paul or by being subjected to public humiliation. After all, it was the first time in recorded history that a boy had broken off with her. It was the first time in recorded history that Diane had not gotten her way. That was probably every bit as traumatic for her as losing her one true love.

I tried to be helpful.

"Diane, these things happen. They happen to everybody."

"Not to me they don't!"

Which was true. Up until then.

But it did happen. And even the people who saw it happen didn't believe it, didn't understand it, couldn't figure it out.

Did I feel sorry for Diane?

She was my friend, after all. Even if no one else felt sorry for her, *I* knew she was suffering. I listened to her suffer, day and night, for two weeks.

But did I feel sorry for Diane?

Well, yes and no.

I *did* feel sorry for Diane.

But on the other hand, I was overjoyed for Miranda Hull.

Loathe at
First Sight

You are dripping on my toes."

"I'm sorry. I was admiring you from afar, and I wanted to admire you from a-near. From afar you looked terrific."

"Oh, thanks a lot. Meaning, up close I look like a toad."

"That's not what I meant at all! You look good up close, too. I love your bathing suit."

"Then why do you keep staring at my toes?"

"It's that stuff you've got on them. What do you call that?"

"Nail polish."

"I know, I know. I meant, what color is it?"

"Rosy Dawn. Look, what is this with my toes?"

"Rosy Dawn. That's kind of romantic. I would have thought it was just pink."

"Will you stop talking about my toes? What are you, weird or something?"

"No! Oh, boy, this whole conversation has

121

gotten off on the wrong foot. Wrong foot—ha! Get it? Foot, toes?"

"Ha ha."

"Just a little humor to lighten up a tense situation. I thought you'd appreciate a good joke."

"I do appreciate a *good* joke."

"I just thought it was too early in our relationship to make personal comments about how great you look in a bathing suit."

"Our relationship? *What* relationship?"

"The one we're going to have."

"Oh, really? Have you always been this unsure of yourself?"

"Have you always been this sarcastic? Look, I just wanted—"

"And besides, toes are personal. Personal comments about toes are just as—as personal as comments about how I look in a bathing suit."

"Well, all right, do you want me to tell you how I think you look in your bathing suit?"

"No. I'm really not interested in your opinion of how I look in my bathing suit."

"Okay, then. How do I look in mine?"

"Wet."

"Picture me dry."

"Please. I already had a nightmare last night."

"That's not very nice."

"Look, I'm sorry, but you just walk up to me, drip on my feet, and start raving about my toes and have the gall to make this incredible assumption that I'm going to be so devastated by your wit and charm—"

"And my good looks."

"—and your *modesty*, that I'll fall madly in love with you."

"Well, actually, I didn't expect you to fall madly in love with me in the first five minutes of our relationship."

"See, that's just what I mean! We don't have a relationship."

"I'm working on it. How'm I doing so far? Say, on a scale of one to ten."

"Minus three. Look, would you please move? You're standing in front of the sun and I'm going to have a big white stripe right in the middle of my back."

"Okay."

"I didn't mean for you to sit down. I meant for you to go away."

"But you didn't get a good look at me yet. All you could see when I was standing up was my knees. They're not necessarily my best feature. This way, you can look straight at me."

"Goody."

"Now, come on. I'm really pretty nice-looking."

"You're really pretty conceited."

"I'm just repeating what other people have told me. Some people think I look a lot like Burt Reynolds."

"Some people think the earth is flat."

"I'm getting this definite impression that you're not being dazzled by my wit and charm."

"How very observant of you."

"That's the first nice thing you've said to me."

"I was being sarcastic."

"I know, but I'm grasping at straws. I thought for sure if the wit and charm didn't work, I could always fall back on my good looks."

"You can fall back on your head, for all I care."

"This isn't going exactly as I planned it. Could we start all over again? Hi, there, my name's Alan. What's yours?"

"Hepzibah."

". . . Hepzibah? . . . I see. And what do your friends call you?"

"Hepzibah."

"Uh, I don't want to insult you or anything,

just in case your name really is Hepzibah, but I have this funny suspicion you're putting me on."

"Flurge."

"I beg your pardon?"

"My last name. Flurge."

"Hepzibah Flurge?"

"Right."

"You're going to burst out laughing any minute, I can tell. Come on, look me straight in the eye and tell me your name is Hepzibah Flurge."

"My name is Hep—Hep—"

"I knew it! You can't even keep a straight face. You can't even say it. . . . You know, you have beautiful eyes. What color are they, exactly?"

"Brown."

"I know, but there are little specks of something in them that—"

"Probably sand."

"Now, come on, don't go all cold and sarcastic on me again. We were doing so well a minute ago."

"I hadn't noticed."

"Sure, you were laughing and everything. Really sort of loosening up, know what I mean? You were right here; you couldn't have missed it. What's your name, really?"

"Anne."

"There, that's better. Mine's Alan."

"You told me."

"I know, but I'm running out of ideas. I did all my best stuff already."

"That was your best stuff? You're in trouble."

"Well, help me out. What kind of a person are you to leave me floundering around for something to say like this? I mean, this is really embarrassing. The least you could do is hold up your end of the discussion."

"I didn't start this ridiculous conversation—if you can even call it a conversation. I don't see why I have to take any responsibility for keeping it up."

"What kind of an attitude is that? What if everybody felt that way? What kind of a world would this be?"

"Quiet."

"Boring."

"Peaceful."

"Not necessarily. If nobody communicated with anybody else there'd be wars all the time."

"There *are* wars all the time."

". . . Uh, yeah. Well. Good point. Would you—um—like me to rub some suntan oil on your shoulders?"

"No, thank you."

"Would you like to rub some on mine?"

"Not particularly."

"Look, Anne, I'm getting desperate here. Where did I go wrong? Did I come on too strong?"

"Yes."

"A little heavy on the wit and charm?"

"Hey, I like wit and charm as much as the next person, but—"

"I overdid it."

"Yes."

"It was the toes, wasn't it? I really turned you off with that stuff about your toes."

"Yes."

"It was just what you call a conversational gambit. You know, an ice-breaker. I mean, not that I don't think your toes are extremely attractive—"

"*Alan*—"

"All right, all right, I swear I'll never mention your toes again. From this minute on, as far as I'm concerned, your toes don't exist. It's just— well, what *should* I have said?"

"What's wrong with hello?"

"Hello? Just hello? But what about after that? What happens after I say hello?"

"Who knows? If you don't try it you'll never find out."

"All right. Here goes. But I don't think this is going to work . . . Hello, Anne."

"Hello, Alan. How's the water?"

"Uh, it's very cold when you first go in, but it warms up after a while."

"A lot of things are like that, don't you think so, Alan?"

"I . . . I think I see what you mean."

"I felt certain you would. . . ."

Your Three Minutes Are Up

And you're sure he was talking about me? You actually heard him say 'Libby Kalman'? I mean, maybe he was talking about Renee Kaplan. Our names sound alike. . . . Sure they do, if you say them fast—"

"Elizabeth, get off that phone!"

Libby held her hand over the mouthpiece and looked pleadingly at her mother. "Just two more minutes, Mom. Just two minutes."

"You've been talking for forty-five minutes already, and your father's expecting—"

"Mother, *please*. This call is really important. It could affect the entire course of my future."

"If you're not off that phone in two minutes you won't *have* a future."

Her mother strode out of the kitchen, her spine ramrod straight, like a soldier. Libby frowned. Whenever her mother squared her shoulders off like that, she meant business. But Libby couldn't worry about that now.

She gazed dreamily at the note pad next to the phone. She'd written the name Mark on it thirteen times. Some Marks were printed in capital letters, some all in small letters. Some she wrote out in her ordinary handwriting, and some she tried to do in elegant italic, like calligraphy.

She wrote the fourteenth Mark in block letters and began shading the *M*.

"But did he know you heard him? I mean, do you think he said it because he knew you were right there and would hear him? And then he'd know you'd tell me, because he knows we're friends? I mean, I think he knows we're friends, doesn't he? Actually, maybe he doesn't. How would he know? . . . You think so? . . . Well, I mean, did he want me to know he said it, or did you just sort of overhear it? . . . Well, because if he knows that I know he said it, he'd expect me to act entirely different than if he didn't know I knew he said it. . . . Sure. And see, if he *didn't* know I knew he said it, and I started acting different, he'd be suspicious, right? And then he'd think, she knows, and what if he really didn't *want* me to know? I mean, you have to deal with a whole other situation, right? Okay, so tell me again, right from the beginning, and don't leave anything out, because even the smallest detail might be—"

"Elizabeth!"

Her father and mother were suddenly looming over her, their faces purple and red—respectively—with rage.

"Get off that phone!" her father roared.

"*Instantly!*" her mother added.

Libby rolled her eyes toward the ceiling. "Look, Stace, I'll have to call you back—"

"You'll call no one back!" her father exploded. "You'll get off that phone and stay off!"

Her mother glared at her, arms folded, face red, shoulders squared. "In two seconds," she said dangerously, "I am going to rip that phone off the wall and *clobber you with it*."

"Uh, Stace, listen, my mother is going berserk here, and my father's about to have a coronary, so I have to get off. Yeah, I know you heard. I'm sure the whole eastern seaboard heard."

Her mother reached for the phone cord.

"Bye, Stace!" Libby slammed the receiver down. "Okay, okay, I'm off."

"I have had it," her father said. "Your mother has had it. Your brother has had it. He'd be here telling you in person he's had it, but he's afraid to come near you because he might kill you, so he's upstairs ripping apart a pillow with his bare hands."

"Fed up, Libby," her mother said. "Absolutely fed up to *here*. You don't own this phone.

There are three other people in the house who need to use it and you haven't shown the slightest consideration for any of us."

"I get business calls, Elizabeth," her father went on. "Important calls. When people can't reach me for three hours, they stop trying. That's bad for business. Bad for my career. Bad for all of us. And I have to *make* calls. And I can't pick up that phone without you hanging over me asking when I'll get off, how long will I take, can I please hurry it up, because you're expecting another vitally important call."

"Well, if you'd just get me my own phone—"

"You can get your own phone when you're earning the money to pay your own phone bill!" her father shouted.

The phone rang. Libby lunged for it, but her father snatched up the receiver before she could get to it.

"No, Libby can't come to the phone now."

Libby's eyes opened wide in horror. "I'm *here*," she whispered desperately. "I'm *right here*."

"No, you'd better try her tomorrow. Sorry."

"How could you *do* that?" Libby cried. "Who was it? Was it a boy or a girl?"

"A boy, I suppose. And I did it because I had to. It's a matter of self-preservation. I'm expecting a very important call—"

"Mark!" Libby wailed. "It was Mark, I just know it. Do you realize what you've done? You've ruined my life, that's all. Just ruined my life. You've destroyed my one chance for happiness. I might as well just go upstairs and swallow everything in the medicine cabinet."

"Good luck with the shaving cream," her mother said drily.

"I can't believe it," Libby said. "I can't believe you did that to me."

"If you can't believe that," her mother said, "you're going to hate this next part."

"What next part?" What could be worse, Libby wondered bitterly, than what her father had already done?

"Look, Libby, I'm sorry, but this business with the phone has gotten completely out of hand." Her mother sat down next to her. "You no sooner get home from school than you're on the phone for three hours with people you've been talking to all day."

"You can't talk to people in *school!*"

"Why not?" her father demanded. "That's ridiculous."

"You just can't," Libby insisted. How could she explain it? It was hopeless to expect her parents to understand what would have been obvious to any teenager.

"Well, you're going to have to," he said, "because from now on you'll have a limit on your calls."

"What do you mean? Like no more than five a day?"

Her father laughed, but it was a short, humorless laugh.

"No, not just the number of calls you make, but the amount of time you spend on each one. Tomorrow I'm getting three egg timers, and I'm going to put one next to each extension. When you make a call, you turn over the egg timer. When the salt runs out of the top, you get off the phone. *Immediately.*"

"How long does it take," Libby asked, her voice weak with shock, "for the salt to run out?"

"Three minutes."

"Three minutes! That's impossible! That's crazy! How can you have a conversation in three minutes?"

Libby's father looked at her thoughtfully. "Look at it this way," he said. "Every time we ask you to get off the phone you say, 'Just two more minutes, just two more minutes.' "

Libby squirmed. He did a pretty good imitation of her.

"So we figure, when the pressure's on, you can wrap up these life-and-death matters in two minutes. When you really have to. We're giving you three minutes—an extra minute more than you always ask for. Anything vitally important that you have to say to anybody can be said in three minutes."

For a moment Libby was too stunned to speak. How could they do this to her? It was humiliating. It was barbaric. There are plenty of vitally important things that can't be said in three minutes. And even if *she* talked fast, what about the person on the other end of the phone? What if he was shy and hesitant and talked slowly, trying to work up his nerve, sort of build up to what he actually called about? Like, say, someone like Mark? Not that Mark would ever call her again, after tonight, but just as an example.

Of course, if they weren't going to limit the number of calls she made—Libby's eyes brightened for a moment. "Then what you're saying is, I have to hold each *individual* call down to three minutes, right?"

Her mother smiled. "Forget it, Libby. No more than three calls a day. You can't just hang up and call back, hang up and call back."

"But what about people who call me?"

"Incoming calls will be timed, too."

"Oh, no! You can't do that! It's not fair! I have *rights*. This is *America*."

"The Constitution," her father said, "does not

give you the inalienable right to a telephone. And we've tried to be understanding and fair, but *you* haven't. We just can't think of any other way to solve this problem."

Dazed, Libby pulled herself out of the chair.

"I can't believe you're doing this to me." She shook her head. "I can't believe my own parents could be so . . . I've got to call Stacey. She'll never believe it either."

"Libby!" her father said. "You can tell Stacey tomorrow. The bad news will wait eight hours."

Libby turned to stare back at him, her face pale with the shock of betrayal. Then she trudged up to her room, shoulders slumping, to do her homework.

What else was there to do?

• •

On the second day after the "Invasion of the Egg Timers," as Libby called it, she thought she'd found a loophole.

"My time is up," she said to Stacey loudly. She looked around furtively, then hunched over the phone. "Wait ten minutes," she whispered, "and call me back."

When the phone rang ten minutes later, Libby grabbed it. "Now look, when I have to get

off, do the same thing again. Wait ten minutes
and call me back."

"This is no way to hold a conversation."

"What can I do?" moaned Libby. "They've
driven me to this."

The third time Stacey called, Libby's mother
got to the phone first:

"Hello, Stacey. Yes, just a minute." She
handed the phone to Libby with a knowing look.
She held up three fingers.

"I know, I know," Libby grumbled. "Three
minutes."

Her mother shook her head. "No. Three
strikes and you're out."

"What?" Libby clamped her hand over the
mouthpiece. "What do you mean?"

"That's the third time Stacey's called. No
more. You may be sticking to the letter of the
law, but you're violating the spirit of it."

"*What?*"

"In plain English: You can't get around it
that way, but nice try."

"Why don't you just lock me in my room and
throw away the key?" Libby wailed. "You're cutting off my lifeline to the outside world!"

Her brother came clumping down the stairs.
"Are you still on that phone?"

"What do you mean, *still?*" Libby demanded. "I haven't even said hello yet."

"Then say hello," said her mother, and carefully turned over the egg timer.

• •

What her parents did to her was bad enough, Libby felt, but what her friends did seemed even a worse betrayal. Within a week after the "Invasion of the Egg Timers," the grumbling started.

"Boy, Libby, you really loused things up for everybody," Renee Kaplan said, sitting down next to her in algebra.

"Me? What did I do?"

"You and those three-minute phone calls. My mother has me on egg timers now."

"But that's not my fault!" Libby said, outraged. "My parents did that, not me!"

"They're *your* parents," Renee said. "It all started with you."

"What all?"

"Suzanne's parents, Lauri's mother—you started an epidemic of egg timers."

"*I* didn't start anything!" Libby couldn't believe it. It was bad enough that her parents had turned on her, but now this? Her friends, too?

"Renee, I'm sorry, but really, it's not fair to blame me. What can I do?"

"Well, if you've got any AT&T stock," Renee said coldly, "I suggest you sell."

••••••••••••••••••••••••

Libby hadn't forgotten about Mark, though she was sure she might as well.

He was in only one of her classes, where he sat way in the back of the room next to his friend John Kelly, so she didn't even get to see him unless she got there early and watched him walk in or hung around after the bell and watched him walk out.

Libby began to think that Stacey had been mistaken—that day she thought she heard Mark talking about Libby, he was actually talking about Renee Kaplan. Either that or her father really *had* ruined everything the night he hung up on Mark, making her sound like a two year old who'd been banished to her room for throwing spinach at the cat.

Why Mark should like her she didn't know. Just because *she* liked him? Just because she thought he was cute? But she did. And he was. And there was no hope for it now, if there ever had been. If, by some remote chance, Mark finally called her one night, he'd barely have enough time to say who it was before she had to hang up. And a shy person like Mark might need a good ten minutes to relax enough to sort of casually work whatever it was he *really* wanted to say into the conversation.

So between rounds of nursing her bruised feelings and snapping at her family, Libby sighed a lot and thought about what was never to be but might have been.

And wrote *Mark* a few hundred times on the memo pad on top of her desk.

•••••••••••••••••••••••

Monday night when the phone rang, Libby didn't even run for it. She was too disheartened. Her spirit had been broken. And it probably wasn't for her, anyhow. Half of her friends had had their phone lines cut off, and most of them blamed it on Libby. Those people who were still speaking to her—mostly the ones who *hadn't* been invaded by egg timers—didn't call her because what kind of a satisfying talk could you have in three minutes?

"It's for you," her brother said, pounding on the door. "Don't forget to turn your timer."

"I won't forget to turn my timer," Libby mimicked. "I probably won't even have to. It's just someone who wants to know what the homework is. That's all we have time to say anymore."

Libby went into her parents' bedroom and picked up the phone.

"Hello," she said dully.

"Uh, hi, Libby?" It was a boy's voice. A boy's shy, hesitant voice.

Libby exhaled so hard she was sure he must have heard her.

The egg timer slipped out of her fingers and rolled under the bed.

"Yes, this is me," she said softly. Wow, did that sound dumb. Well, what could you expect? She wasn't getting much practice in the art of telephone conversation lately.

"It's Mark Welch. Uh"—he cleared his throat—"I know you can't stay on the phone very long. . . ."

The whole world knows my problems, Libby thought bitterly. This is humiliating.

"So I'll—uh—get right to the point."

He probably wants to know what the homework is in earth science, Libby thought.

"You know they're having this—uh—Sixties Dance in school next Saturday, and I was wondering if you'd—I mean, I don't dance really well or anything, but—well, you know, if you want to—"

I don't believe it! Libby thought. I'm going to faint. Faint later! she told herself. Your three minutes are almost up. She felt for her heart; it was still beating. Very rapidly.

"I mean, what I thought was maybe we could go, you know, together, if you want."

"That would be really nice," Libby said. How calm she sounded! Just as if Mark called her every day! Just as if she hadn't been waiting and hoping for weeks for this moment. "I'd really like that."

"You would?" Mark sounded like he couldn't believe it. Like he'd expected her to say no. "Oh, good. Great. I'll pick you up about eight, okay?"

"Eight is fine."

"Well. Well, okay. I guess you have to get off now."

"Right, right," Libby said, dazed. "I guess I'd better. Bye."

"Bye. Take care."

Libby dropped the receiver back on the hook and threw herself across her parents' bed. *Now* she was going to faint. She was going to faint from shock and then die of happiness.

No. Not yet.

First she had to call Stacey.

"Stace? Stace, you're not going to believe this—"

"He called?" Stacey asked excitedly. "Did he call yet?"

"What? How did you know—"

"He did call! Did he ask you?"

"Stacey, how do you know all this?" Libby demanded.

"John sort of hinted around at it—I wormed most of it out of him."

"Why didn't you tell me?"

"Because John said he was so nervous about it he might chicken out at the last minute, and I didn't want to get your hopes up for nothing. But he really called?"

"Yes," sighed Libby. "Yesss. . . ."

"Well, it's really bizarre, Lib. Listen, you're not going to believe this. He tried to call you for two weeks."

"What?"

"But your line was always busy." Stacey giggled. "Isn't that ironic?"

"What?"

"And he was too shy to talk to you in school, with people all around. And when he finally did reach you, your father said you couldn't come to the phone. So he gave up. He figured you were so popular you'd never go out with him. All those phone calls and all."

"What?"

"You're repeating yourself, Libby. So anyhow, when this thing with the time limit came up, he figured he'd be able to get you now, but he was still sure you wouldn't be interested in him. It took a whole week for John to help him work up the nerve to try."

In a haze, Libby slid off the bed and down to the floor. Still holding onto the receiver, she groped around under the bed till she found the egg timer. She put it down carefully on the night table.

"Libby? You still there?"

"Yeah, I'm still here. My time's almost up, though. I don't believe this."

"I told you you wouldn't. Oh, Lib, did you die? Were you surprised? I would have died."

"No, no, I'm saving that for later," Libby said distractedly.

Her mother walked into the room. She looked at the egg timer, which had never been turned over, and saw that all the salt was on the bottom, as if it had run out. She stared pointedly at Libby.

"I have to go, Stace. Talk to you later. I mean, tomorrow."

"Okay. Take care."

Libby hung up the phone and walked dreamily toward the door.

She paused just before leaving the bedroom and looked at her mother almost fondly.

"You know," she murmured, "you might be right."

"About what?" her mother asked, startled.

Libby trailed her fingers gently around the doorknob.

"Maybe you *can* say anything you have to say in three minutes . . . if it's important enough."

Double
Date

arole, he noticed me! He
.... C said something!"

"Hallelujah! What'd he say?"

" 'Can I help you find something?' "

There was a short silence at the other end of the phone.

"That's it?"

"Well, it's something, isn't it? I mean, he could have left me floundering around there in the middle of the aspirin—"

"I suppose. So, what did you say?"

"The only thing I could think of. I asked him what the best buy on aspirin was. He said he didn't know, he was only a stock clerk. But look, if he's just a stock clerk he didn't even have to bother, right? They have salespeople to help customers. He didn't have to offer to help me."

"He didn't help you," Carole pointed out.

"I know, but he noticed me. That's the main thing. And next time . . ."

"What about next time?"

"I don't know yet. But I'll think of something. Knock over the Pampers display. Run barefoot through the corn and callus removers—*something*. How's it going on your end?"

"I thought you'd never ask." Carole sighed. "Janie, you're not going to believe this, but he sat down next to me on the bus this afternoon."

"That's great! Did he say anything?"

"Well, no, but—"

"Did you say anything?"

"Oh, Janie, how could I? I mean, when he sat down right next to me like that I was paralyzed. I mean, I couldn't *move*. And he didn't have to sit next to me. There were at least three other empty seats on the bus."

"Well, keep up the good work," I said encouragingly.

"But I didn't *do* anything."

"You will next time. Just like I will. Okay?"

"I definitely promise. Next time I'll make the big move."

"Me, too," said Carole.

Carole and I had been best friends since the third grade, and it was driving us crazy now that we weren't in the same school anymore. We weren't that far apart—her parents had moved to a house right on the water—but we were in different school districts now, after having gone all the way through junior high school together. It was really hard.

We talked almost every day on the phone, and I still thought of her as my best friend, but I could see what would happen. She was making new friends in her new school, and we managed to get together less and less often. I was afraid it was only a matter of time before we would drift apart and find other best friends to tell everything to.

Only I didn't know where I'd ever find another friend like Carole.

••••••••••••••••••••••••

A couple of days later I went back to the drugstore. I didn't want to rush it. I mean, I didn't want to be too obvious, running to the drugstore every day and hanging around waiting for him to spot me. And besides, it took me almost that long to think up something I wanted to buy; that is, something I wouldn't mind having him *see* me buy. There are only a certain number of things in a drugstore you can let a boy see you buying without getting embarrassed.

Finally I came up with the perfect thing. Suntan oil.

One of the things that was perfect about it was that it was October, and they hadn't had displays of suntan stuff for two months, so I'd have to ask him for it. And he'd wonder why I wanted suntan oil in October. The other thing that was perfect about it was that I wouldn't be embarrassed buying it.

He was unloading a carton of disposable lighters when I walked in. I just stood there a moment and watched him. He had dark blond hair and these incredibly intense blue eyes. . . . When I asked him about the suntan oil, I thought they would pierce right through me.

"Yeah, I think we still have some. Aisle three. We don't get much call for it this time of year."

Ask me why I want it, I begged him silently. Go on, I've got my answer all planned. For a moment I stood there, gazing at him, willing him to ask me why I wanted suntan oil in October. I was just about to give up when he looked over the box of lighters, gazed straight back into my eyes, and said, "Still working on your tan, huh?"

"Not exactly." It took all the courage I had to say my next line. "But I love walking on the beach in the fall, don't you?"

"You don't need suntan oil in the fall, do you?"

That wasn't what he was supposed to say. He was supposed to say, "Yes, I love walking on the beach in the fall, too. In fact, I was going to go walking on the beach this weekend. If you're not doing anything . . ."

" . . . unless," he was saying, "you get windburned."

Windburned is very unromantic. He was studying my face now. I began to shift my feet, feeling self-conscious, and not liking the idea of him picturing what I'd look like with a windburn. But liking *very much* the way those deep blue eyes surveyed me.

Even if it did make me self-conscious.

"No, no, I need it for my nose."

Which made him fix his gaze on my nose.

I hadn't planned on this either. In fact, I hadn't planned on anything past "I love walking on the beach in the fall, too." I just figured when he asked if I wasn't doing anything that weekend, I'd say I'd love to go walking on the beach with him, and things would just naturally progress from there.

He grinned. "Gets red, huh?"

A red nose is even more unromantic than a windburn. But he had such a warm smile, such an infectious grin, such blue, blue eyes . . .

I hardly even minded spending $2.59 for suntan oil I'd never use.

••••••••••••••••••••••••

"Oh, Janie, you'll never believe it. We had the first meeting of *Driftwood* today. You know, the literary magazine. And I walked in with a bunch of my poems and there he was!"

"You mean, he's on the magazine, too? He writes? Carole, that's fantastic."

"No, not exactly. I mean, he doesn't write. He's going to be the business manager. You know, sell ads and take care of the financial stuff."

"Oh." Carole is a really terrific poet. "Well, but that's great, too. I mean, both of you working on the magazine."

"And you know what? I think he remembered me from the bus."

"Did he say so?"

"No, but he said, 'Hi, there.' Just like that."

"Just like that?"

"You know—like he wasn't saying it for the first time. Like he was recognizing me."

"Oh, yeah, I see what you mean." I did, sort of. I sighed. "Oh, Carole, I wish I could see him. And I wish you could see mine. This is awful, being in different schools."

"I know," she said sadly. "I wish you could see him, too. He's so cute. Those beautiful blue eyes." She must have said that about his eyes ten times since she'd first seen him.

"Mine, too," I said. For the tenth time.

"And his name is Richard." She breathed it out like a sigh.

"Well, you beat me. I still don't know mine's name."

"Why don't you ask him?"

"I can't come right out and ask him; I mean, he's just this guy who works in the drugstore. So far. I'm waiting for *him* to ask *me*."

••••••••••••••••••••••••

How long, I wondered, could I stand there in the stationery aisle, debating over a box of paper clips? There was an open carton of yellow legal pads on the floor. It was half unpacked, so I assumed he had to come back sometime and unpack the rest of it, but when? I'd been there so long the manager was probably beginning to think I was casing the joint.

I picked up and put back several different kinds of ballpoint pens. At least that looked more realistic than trying to make a decision about paper clips. Especially since they only had one kind on the shelves.

"Hey, it's you! Walked on the beach yet?"

I whirled around and three plastic pens spun out of my hand. He was practically at my elbow and I hadn't even seen him coming.

I bent down to pick up the pens. I felt stupid

and clumsy, but gathering them up at least gave me something to do while I tried to think of something to say.

I stood up and forced a casual smile. "My nose isn't red, is it?"

"No. But your cheeks are a little flushed."

Oh, my. I could feel them getting flushed-er. I turned away and stuck the pens back on the shelf.

I cleared my throat and turned back to him. "Actually," I said bravely, "I don't drive, so it's kind of hard to get to the beach. In the fall, nobody wants to go with me."

There went that grin again. But this time it was almost sly, knowing.

"I can't believe," he said softly, "that no one wants to take you to the beach."

Flushed-er and flushed-er. I stared down at plastic bags of rubber bands. At the legal pads. At six different kinds of glue.

"I, for instance, would love to take you to the beach."

Six different kinds of glue swam before my eyes. The lines on the legal pads got all wavy. Was it awfully warm in here, or was it just Indian summer?

"I—uh—don't even know you. I mean, I don't even know your name. Or anything."

He pointed to a little plastic badge on his blue store jacket. Why hadn't I ever noticed it before? Because I was too busy looking into his blue eyes to notice his blue jacket, that's why.

"And I'm perfectly respectable. Ask anybody. Come on." He took my arm and sort of pulled me along to the front of the store. "Ask Marcia. Marcia, hey!"

The cashier at the front counter turned around.

"Marcia, tell—tell—hey, what's *your* name?"

"Jane," I whispered.

"Jane," he repeated. "Marcia, tell Jane here that I'm perfectly respectable. That she'd be absolutely safe letting me take her to the beach."

Marcia smiled. "He's perfectly respectable," she said. Marcia was at least thirty and looked very respectable herself. "He's worked here six months and hasn't stolen a thing. Really, Dick's a very nice—" Suddenly she started to laugh.

"You *have* to go out with him," Marcia said. "You really have to. It's kismet."

"What do you mean?" he asked.

"Dick and Jane." She couldn't stop laughing. "Dick and Jane, for heaven's sake. Hey, where are Spot and Puff?"

I thought she was acting pretty silly for a

thirty-year-old woman, but Dick started to laugh, too, so it must have been funny.

"You see," he said, "you really have to let me take you to the beach. We can't disappoint Marcia. Or kismet."

"I guess not," I said. But I wondered, briefly, who was going to explain kismet to my mother.

....

"Carole, I've been trying to get you for days."

It was happening, just like I knew it would. Carole and I were growing apart, as she got caught up in the whirl of her new school.

"I've been trying to get you for days, too. We keep missing each other."

"But listen to what—"

"The most incredible—"

We said it together and laughed. "You first," I said, even though I was dying to tell her about my Sunday afternoon at the beach.

"We went to the movies!" she said triumphantly.

"Carole! You didn't even tell me he asked you!"

"I tried. But you were never home when I called. I guess, what with *Driftwood* and orchestra rehearsals and chorus I couldn't try all that often. Anyway, we went last Saturday night."

"What did you see?"

"*Motel Macabre*. And believe me, I didn't see that much of it. I had my hands over my eyes practically through the whole thing. It was really disgusting."

"Sounds great," I said drily.

"Yeah, it was. Richard kept telling me what was happening while I had my hands over my eyes."

"Not in great detail, I hope."

"No, he sort of told me the expurgated version. He was so sweet. We're going out next Saturday, too. They're having an All-time Great Gore Festival at the Triplex. Four of the gruesomest movies of all time."

"I didn't know you liked that stuff," I said, puzzled.

"Well, I really don't, but who cares? It's nice to be scared with Richard right there next to me. Now, what's happening at the drugstore?"

I told her the whole thing, right up to the walk on the beach and the drive home and how much he impressed my parents.

"But you hate the beach!" Carole said. "Why did you tell him you liked the beach? You burn to a crisp and then you peel and half the time you get sun poisoning—"

"Yeah, well, once I dreamed up that bit with

the suntan oil I was sort of stuck with it. I don't care. He's very mature. I think he's in college. You should have seen how he was with my father—"

"You *think* he's in college? Don't you know?"

"Well, no, actually it didn't come up. He's taking me out on his boat next week."

"His boat? In this weather? Janie, you don't even swim!"

"With any luck," I said dreamily, "I'll fall overboard, and he'll have to rescue me and give me mouth-to-mouth resuscitation."

••••••••••••••••••••••••••

Weeks flew by before I knew they were gone. I tried to call Carole several times, and my mother told me she'd called me, but our schedules never seemed to jibe. I was seeing Dick regularly, when he didn't have to work. Real dates, sometimes on Saturday nights, sometimes Sundays, whenever he could get the car.

I only went to the drugstore now when I had to, even though I would have liked to see him every day. I didn't want to seem too eager, to hang on him. I didn't want him to get tired of me, tired of going with me, tired of kissing me, tired of holding my hand.

What with Dick and school and drama club

rehearsals and my other friends—and Carole with *her* boyfriend and *her* friends and *her* school—I realized it was probably only a matter of time till we ended up speaking to each other maybe twice a year and exchanging Christmas cards.

Which struck me as so sad and so ridiculous, since we were barely ten miles apart, that I called her every day for a week until I reached her, determined that we were going to see each other without letting another weekend go by.

"Yes!" she yelled into the phone. "Absolutely! Oh, Jane, I am *dying* to see you. Maybe Richard could even drive me over, if he can get the car. If not, my mother or father. And if nobody can, I'll walk!"

"Oh, I hope Richard can drive you. I'd love to meet him."

"You'd love him, Janie, you really would. But at least I'll get to meet Dick—even if I have to go buy suntan lotion to do it!"

"Hey, Carole, isn't that funny? I just realized—both our boyfriends are named Richard. I mean, Dick is a nickname for Richard."

"That really is bizarre," Carole said. "How come we never realized that before?"

"I guess all I could think about was Dick and Jane." I giggled.

Carole laughed. "And besides, we always did have the same taste in boys."

••••••••••••••••••••••••••

Carole's mother drove her over late Saturday afternoon, and we jumped around and hugged each other and screamed like five year olds right on the front lawn in the cold November dusk.

"It's been years!" Carole shrieked.

"Decades!"

"Centuries!"

"Since August!" I screamed, and we practically fell over each other, laughing.

My mother said we had an hour till dinner.

"Good," said Carole. "Let's go to the drugstore. I need some suntan oil."

We started screeching again, and I grabbed my jacket out of the closet and ran out the front door.

"I can see *you* all weekend," Carole said. "But first I have to see this gorgeous hunk of yours. I hope he'll still be there."

"Oh, yeah, he has to work tonight. It's perfect timing."

"I'm warning you, I'm prejudiced. I have a gorgeous hunk of my own, you know."

"Well, maybe someday we could double-date with our respective hunks, and—and—"

We started giggling like babies again and linked arms.

"Respective hunks," Carole cackled. Everything struck us as funny; even our breath coming out all frosty smoke seemed hysterical.

We got to the drugstore and stood outside a minute trying to sober up. We knew we looked like a pair of staggering drunks, but every time we tried to stop giggling and put on airs of quiet dignity and composure—or at least maturity—we started howling all over again.

People coming out of the store into the parking lot made wide detours around us, which made us laugh even harder.

"Okay, now look, this is it," I said sternly. "Finished. *Finito. Finis.* I am absolutely serious. See how serious I—"

Carole started to giggle again, but suddenly the door opened and Dick came out, zipping up his suede jacket.

"Dick!" I said delightedly.

He turned toward us, and I swear, even in the red light from the store sign, I could see his face turn white.

"Richard!" Carole sounded like she was choking.

He just stood there a moment, his back pressed against the door, his eyes wide with shock.

Slowly, Carole and I turned our heads toward each other.

"Dick?" she whispered incredulously.

"Richard?" I could hardly say the name.

Suddenly we heard a voice calling from the parking lot.

"Rick! Rick! Here I am!"

He looked past us. We turned around and saw a girl with long blond hair standing by a car under one of the light poles. She was waving at him.

The next thing we knew, he was sprinting across the parking lot toward the girl with the long blond hair.

· ·

We spent the rest of the weekend huddled in my room, taking turns crying. When we got too tired to cry, we compared notes.

"Richard always—"

"Dick never—"

"Oh, Janie, I really loved him!"

"I thought he really loved *me!*"

We wondered if we should hate each other. We wondered who the girl with the long blond hair was. We wondered when he'd found the time for *her.* We wondered how we could have known so little about Dick/Richard/Rick, when we thought we knew him so well.

It was the weirdest, eeriest twenty-four hours either of us had ever spent. And when Carole went home Sunday night, I went up to my room and cried some more. Alone.

I was sure she did the same.

Maybe we should have resented each other, but somehow it didn't work out that way. Our mutual love for Richard/Dick turned into mutual hate, so I guess we were able to turn all our resentment onto him, where it belonged.

Carole and I see much more of each other now, and we talk at least once a week on the phone.

So, I suppose, if I wanted to be charitable and positive and find a way to look at the experience— and Dick—in the best possible light, I could say that in a strange, painful way, he brought Carole and me closer together. Maybe even saved our friendship.

But no matter how hard I try, I can't bring myself to say one charitable word about Marcia.

About the Author

Ellen Conford is the author of books such as *We Interrupt This Semester for an Important Bulletin* and *Dear Lovey Hart, I Am Desperate* (both available as Scholastic paperbacks). Conford's uncannily accurate stories have been delighting teenage audiences for years. She lives, writes, and eats spaghetti in Great Neck, New York.